THE IRVING FILE
AN AUNT BESSIE COLD CASE MYSTERY
BOOK NINE

DIANA XARISSA

Copyright © 2023 by DX Dunn, LLC

Cover Copyright © 2023 Tell-Tale Book Covers

Cover Photo Copyright © 2019 Kevin Moughtin

ISBN: 9798367279955

All rights reserved.

No part of this publication may be reproduced, distributed, or transmitted in any form or by any means, including photocopying, recording, or other electronic or mechanical methods, without the prior written permission of the publisher, except as permitted by U.S. copyright law. For permission requests, contact diana@dianaxarissa.com

The story, all names, characters, and incidents portrayed in this production are fictitious. No identification with actual persons (living or deceased), places, buildings, and products is intended or should be inferred.

First edition 2023

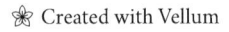

❀ Created with Vellum

CHAPTER 1

"Good afternoon," Andrew said from the head of the table. He smiled at Bessie, who was sitting on his right. "Before we start talking about our next case, I need to introduce you all to a friend of mine. This is Kenneth Hamilton." Andrew gestured towards the dark-haired man on his left.

Kenneth grinned. "Call me Ken," he said.

Everyone around the table nodded, and a few people said "hello."

"Ken and I worked together at Scotland Yard for several years," Andrew continued. "After the considerable success of our cold case unit here, he's been tasked with setting up a similar unit back in London. I invited him to join us this month so that he could see for himself exactly how our unit functions."

"You don't just function, though," Ken said. "You work magic. You've considered eight cold cases over eight months, and you've solved every single one of them. I've already warned my supervisor in London that she shouldn't expect that sort of success from my unit."

Andrew nodded. "We've been surprisingly successful. When we started, I hoped that we'd solve one case in ten. I expect we're due for a run of cases that we can't solve, but I continue to be hopeful every time we start looking at a new case."

"Some of our luck should be credited to Andrew's selection process," Harry suggested. "He has a real talent for finding cases that should have been solved previously."

A few people around the table nodded.

"Ken and I have spent several days going over the criteria that I use when selecting cases," Andrew replied.

"And I've taken pages and pages of notes," Ken added. "My unit has a number of restrictions that don't apply to yours, though, or it will initially. We're going to be limited to murder investigations for incidents that took place in London. If we can solve a few of those, we might be given permission to consider other types of cases, or cases in other parts of the United Kingdom."

"Who else is in the unit?" Charles asked.

"That's a very good question," Ken replied. "I'm still working on that, actually. I'd love to have you and Harry, but my unit is going to be working full-time on our cold cases, and I know neither of you is interested in going back to police work on a full-time basis."

Harry laughed. "I work harder now than I did when I worked full-time. Between this unit and my consulting work, I haven't had a day off in over a year."

"And you wouldn't have it any other way," Charles said.

Harry nodded. "I love what I do, and I'd like to think I'm making a difference."

Andrew cleared his throat. "I'm going to have Ken introduce himself properly, and then I'd like all of you to introduce yourselves. As he said, Ken is still building his team. I want him to appreciate the interesting diversity of our little group."

Bessie glanced at her friends around the table. "Interesting diversity" was one way of describing them.

Ken cleared his throat. "As Andrew said, I'm Ken Hamilton. I'm fifty-seven years old and I'm single. My ex-wife and I have two children, both of whom are on their own now. She's remarried and much happier than she was when she and I were together. I'm quite happy being single. I joined the police right out of school and then got my degree through the Open University. I worked with Andrew for a few years before he retired. Since then, I've mostly moved into administration, pushing papers around rather than chasing criminals. While I don't miss a lot of being on the street, I am looking forward to getting back to investigating with my new unit. I just hope we can achieve a tiny fraction of the success of this unit."

"One in ten cases would be a good average," Andrew told him.

"I know, and I've set that as my goal. My supervisor has loftier ambitions, of course."

"They always do," Harry said with a laugh.

"I'd like you each to introduce yourselves in a similar fashion to what Ken just did," Andrew said. "That includes those of you who know Ken. I want him to have brief bios for each of you that he can use when considering the structure of his own team."

Harry nodded. "That makes sense. I'm Harry Blake, retired Scotland Yard inspector. Never married. No children. My area of expertise is murder, and I never shied away from dealing with the most brutal and horrific examples."

"We've met only once or twice before," Ken said. "But you're a legend in the field."

Harry shrugged. "I just try to do my job as best I can." He looked at Charles, who was next to him.

"Oh, Charles Morris. Like Andrew and Harry, I'm retired from Scotland Yard. Over my time there, I became something of an expert in missing person cases. I now operate as a consultant for those sorts of cases all over the world."

"Marriages? Children?" Harry prompted him.

"Neither," Charles replied flatly.

"Speaking of legends," Ken said. "I can't tell you how many hours I've spent studying just a handful of your missing person cases. I believe I've nearly memorised every word in the file for the Boland case."

Charles flushed. "That was an interesting case. I knew there was something suspicious about the maid and the cook, but I wasn't entirely certain that whatever they were doing was actually tied to the missing woman or not."

"And, of course, it was, and you were able to rescue Katrina Boland," Ken said.

"There's more to the story than what's in the file," Charles told him.

"Really?" Ken asked.

Charles grinned. "The maid also had a connection to the man across the street."

"Paul Porter?"

"You truly have memorised the file. Paul was only tangentially connected to the case."

"I've always wondered why he was outside in his garden at midnight," Ken replied.

Charles nodded. "That's part of the story." He looked around the table and laughed. "No one else has any idea what we're going on about. Let's talk later, over a drink."

"I'd like that," Ken said.

"Next?" Andrew asked, looking at John, who was sitting next to Charles, sipping tea.

"Ah, yes, of course," John replied, putting his cup down. "I'm John Rockwell. I'm an inspector with the Isle of Man Constabulary. I'm probably twenty years or more away from retirement, but I also love my job and can't imagine retiring. I was married once. That marriage ended in divorce. My ex-wife, Sue, and I had two children together, Thomas and Amy. They're both in their teens and they live with me, following their mother's unexpected passing."

"She died in Africa, on her honeymoon, I believe," Ken said.

John nodded. "Her second husband, Harvey, had always wanted to travel to Africa. He's a doctor, and he'd always wanted to use his skills to help people in developing countries."

"If you don't mind my asking, what happened to Sue? Was she in an accident there?" Ken asked.

"I wish I knew," John replied with a shake of his head. "I was told that she fell ill with some sort of fever. I have every reason to believe that Harvey was negligent in getting her treatment, but I can't prove anything from here. The authorities where they were staying have been politely unhelpful."

"And I believe Harvey is still there, saving lives in small villages all over the country," Ken said.

"He is. I've made it clear that when he does finally return to the UK, he's going to have to answer a great many questions," John replied grimly. "I'm going to do everything in my power to have him detained and questioned extensively, but I suspect no matter what I do, I'll never actually know what happened to Sue."

"Is Harvey planning to return to the UK?" Andrew asked.

John shrugged. "I don't know. I don't have any contact with the man, and neither do the children. He was their stepfather for only a very short amount of time and neither of them cared for him, so that isn't surprising. I've been told that his passport has been flagged so that he will be detained as soon as he tries to re-enter the UK, but that's all I know."

"Edward Bennett arranged that for you, didn't he?" Andrew asked.

"He did," John confirmed.

"Harvey isn't dumb enough to come back," Doona said. "He'll stay in Africa for the rest of his life, or maybe he'll move somewhere else altogether, like the US or Canada."

John patted Doona's shoulder and then looked at Andrew. "Is there anything else I should add?" he asked.

Andrew laughed. "It's your life story you're meant to be sharing."

John thought for a minute. "I'll just add that being a part of this unit has been both educational and fascinating. I hope that we continue to solve cases, but I would still be a part of the unit even if we were solving only one or two cases a year, as Andrew expected. Being able to work with Harry, Charles, and Andrew is a real highlight of my career."

Ken nodded. "It's nice to meet you."

"Likewise," John replied. He glanced at Doona and then back at Ken. "I should also tell you that I'm currently sharing my life with a very special woman. You're going to meet her next. Doona and I are still working out exactly where our relationship is going, but I can't imagine my life without her by my side."

Doona flushed and then blinked several times. Bessie grinned. It was unusual for either of them to talk about their relationship. She was delighted to hear that John felt so strongly about her closest friend.

"And how do I follow that?" Doona asked, laughing a bit shakily. "I think I'll just ignore that part for now and talk about other things. I'm Doona Moore. I've had lots of different jobs over the years, but my last job was as a receptionist at the Laxey Constabulary. I'm more or less retired now, even though I'm too young to be properly retired. Although I'm not really retired at all. I actually work incredibly hard from home."

She stopped and took a deep breath. "I'm babbling because I'm feeling rather overwhelmed by what John said," she admitted. "Let me start over."

"Feel free to babble," Ken told her. "I'm fascinated."

Doona blushed. "More like amused but trying to be polite. But in order to understand my current job, you need to know about my marriages. I've been married twice. The first time, I married my first boyfriend. It seemed like the thing we were supposed to do next, so that's what we did. It didn't take us both long to realise that we weren't happy together, though. We went through a very friendly divorce, and I get together with him and his wife once in a while for dinner or drinks. They have a few very badly behaved children that I see as little as possible."

Ken chuckled. "The children should improve as they get older."

"I've not seen any signs of improvement yet, but I'm sure their parents live in hope," Doona replied. "My second marriage was a bit more complicated. Charles was only visiting the island, but he managed to sweep me off my feet and persuade me to marry him. Not long after our honeymoon, I found out that he was cheating. I started divorce proceedings, but hadn't managed to complete them before Charles's untimely death."

"Ah, this is when you met Andrew, isn't it?" Ken asked. "He told me something about all of this. You were at a holiday park in the UK when your husband was murdered. Am I remembering that correctly?"

Doona nodded. "Charles had tricked me into visiting the park, but that's another story. After his death, once the killer was caught, I found out that Charles had named me as his heir. I was the beneficiary of several life insurance policies, and I also inherited fractional shares in hospitality businesses around the UK. I sold nearly everything, only retaining fifty per cent ownership in the holiday park you mentioned earlier."

"I understand those places are very profitable," Ken said.

"I wish," Doona replied. "Don't get me wrong, it is profitable, but at the moment my partner and I are reinvesting nearly all of the profits back into the park. There are literally hundreds of buildings on the site, and most of them need painting and updating." She sighed and then shook her head. "Don't get me started. I'll just add that I spend nearly all of my time trying to manage the park from here, which isn't easy. I spent ten days there last month, and I'll be heading back once this week's cold case unit meetings are finished. June is the start of our busiest season, and the park needs all of their management on site as much as possible."

Ken nodded. "I hope you get to enjoy the park at least some of the time."

"I do, and John will be bringing the children over for a few weeks later in the summer, too, which will be nice. I'm just struggling to decide whether I should keep my share of the park and keep working hard at managing it or sell my share to my partner and let him have all of the hassle," Doona told him.

"You know you can miss a month of cold case meetings if you need to," Andrew told her.

Doona quickly shook her head. "Being a part of this unit makes me feel as if I'm making a difference in the world. I truly don't think anyone cares what colour the walls in their holiday cottage are, but I still have to spend hours every day arguing about shades of beige with my partner and the park's manager. Not only does this unit make me feel useful, but it's also a great distraction from the myriad stupid decisions I have to make every day for the park."

"Well, it's very nice to meet you," Ken told her. "And I'll admit that I'm fascinated by the idea of owning a holiday park. If you ever want to talk about it, let me know."

"She doesn't ever want to talk about it," John said with a grin.

Doona chuckled. "The thing is, I spend most of my time on the phone, talking about so many details that when I'm done, I don't want to talk about it. I'm also grumpy and annoying, and I've no idea why John puts up with me, but I'm enormously grateful that he does." She put her hand over his.

John looked at her and smiled. "She's worth a fortune," he told Ken.

Doona laughed loudly. "He hates my money and won't let me spend any on him or his children. We're working that out, though."

"I'm learning to choose my battles," John explained. "The kids tend to take Doona's side, especially if it means her buying something for them."

"I never particularly wanted children, but I can't imagine loving Thomas and Amy more if they were my own," Doona said, looking down at the table. "Spoiling them a little bit is one of my life's greatest pleasures."

John leaned over and kissed the top of Doona's head. "Love you," he said softly.

"Snap," she replied.

After an awkward moment, Andrew cleared his throat. "Right, let's move on. Hugh is next."

Hugh nodded. "I'm Hugh Watterson, and I'm a constable with the Laxey Constabulary. I joined the police right out of school, and I didn't think I'd ever take another class again. Now I'm studying at the local college, working on getting the qualifications I'll need to become an inspector one day."

"Good for you," Ken said.

"I, well, I was pretty lazy when I was younger, but a couple of things happened that changed all of that. First, John arrived on the island. When he took over the Laxey branch of the Constabulary, he started working with all of the constables, encouraging us to work hard and learn as much as we could. I'd never had a supervisor take such an interest in me before."

"I could see a lot of potential," John told him.

Hugh flushed. "At the same time, I met someone special. Grace used to be a teacher at a Douglas primary school. She's beautiful and really smart, much smarter than I am. It took me ages to work up the nerve to ask her to marry me, but when I did, she actually said yes. That's when I started thinking about going back to school, but I didn't do anything about it until after Aalish arrived. I could talk all afternoon about my daughter, who is the most amazing thing in the entire world, but I don't expect everyone to share my enthusiasm for her, even though they should."

Everyone laughed.

"You have a lot on your plate, then, with school, your job, this unit, and a baby at home," Ken suggested.

"I do, but it's worth it. I'll sleep when I'm older," Hugh replied.

"You're still in your twenties?" Ken asked.

Hugh nodded. "And I can't imagine giving up any of those things. Being a part of this unit is especially important to me. We're doing amazing things here, and I feel fortunate every day to have been given a chance to be a part of it."

"You earned your spot here, the same as everyone else," Andrew told him. He looked at Bessie. "Your turn," he said.

Bessie flushed as everyone at the table looked at her. "I'm Elizabeth Cubbon, but everyone calls me Bessie. I've lived on the island for all of my adult life, although I did spend my childhood in the US. I've never married or had children. I suppose I'm here because several years ago now I stumbled across a dead body on the beach near my home. That was just the first of many murder investigations in which I found myself involved. Since the cold case unit has started meeting, the instances of dead bodies turning up on the island seem to have stopped. I hope it stays that way."

Ken nodded. "I spent some time reading through some of the cases in which you were involved. It's fascinating to me how sometimes crimes seem to come in clusters in that way."

"And I'm Andrew Cheatham," Andrew said with a grin. "Retired Scotland Yard inspector. Author of several books on investigative techniques. Bored old man with too much time on my hands and a burning desire to get away from my family as often as possible."

Ken laughed. "Your daughter is lovely."

Andrew shrugged. "Helen is staying with me again this month. Ken and Helen and I flew to the island together this morning. She was charming to him, of course," he told the others.

"And she's always been incredibly pleasant when I've spent time with her," Bessie added. "I enjoyed showing her around the island last month."

"I know, and I need to be more appreciative of her efforts, since if she weren't able to accompany me to the island, we'd have to have these meetings in London, and I don't think anyone wants to do that," Andrew replied.

"I wouldn't mind having an occasional meeting in London," Doona said.

"We would make it work if we had to," John added.

"But Charles and I have come to appreciate the island's charms," Harry said.

"I even found myself looking forward to staying on Laxey Beach again," Charles said.

"That's a problem for later," Andrew said. "There aren't any additional cottages available on the beach, so we need to find somewhere for Ken to stay."

"I don't suppose there are any rooms available here," Bessie said.

"Unfortunately, the Seaview is also fully booked," Andrew replied. "I rang half a dozen different hotels before we flew across, and everywhere I rang was full. We may have to spend the rest of the day trying to find somewhere for him."

"Charles and I both have spare rooms in our cottages," Harry said, sounding anything but enthusiastic about the idea of sharing with Ken.

"That may be our only option," Andrew said. "But we'll worry about that after the meeting. I'm sure you're all eager to talk about the case we're going to be considering this month."

"Indeed," Bessie murmured. She picked up her pen and opened her notebook to a blank page, ready to start taking notes.

CHAPTER 2

"Ken, for your benefit, I'll explain a bit about how I manage the unit," Andrew began. "I always give everyone a very brief introduction to the case, sharing only the bare minimum of information. Then I give out copies of the case file. People can read those at their leisure. We meet as a group again a day or two later to discuss the case."

"When you say bare minimum, how bare?" Ken asked.

"You'll see in a minute," Andrew replied. "I give them the basic facts about the case. Sometimes I provide them with a list of the main suspects as well."

"Which helps me keep them all straight in my head as I read the case file," Bessie interjected.

Ken nodded. "That makes sense."

"I'll be giving you a copy of the case file, too," Andrew told Ken. "And you are more than welcome to share your thoughts on the case as we work through it."

"Thanks for that, but I don't want to do anything that might interfere with the group dynamic," Ken replied.

"The group dynamic is far less important than solving

cases," Andrew said firmly. "But let's get started. We're going to New Zealand this time."

"New Zealand?" Doona repeated. "I've always wanted to visit there. It always looks so wonderful in pictures."

"It wasn't so wonderful for Larry Irving five years ago," Andrew replied.

Bessie wrote the name in her notebook.

"Where in New Zealand?" Ken asked. "I've been there," he added when Andrew looked over at him.

"Wellington."

Ken shrugged. "I spent a weekend there on my way to Australia. It's a lovely city, or it was twenty-something years ago."

"But the murder took place five years ago?" Charles asked.

"Yes, almost exactly five years ago," Andrew replied. "Amelia Irving, who was thirty-five at the time, came home from a business trip and found her husband dead. She rang the police as soon as she found the body."

"Where was the body?" Hugh asked.

"In their bedroom. Amelia's flight landed not long after six at night, so it was dark by the time she got her bags and got a taxi to her house. She rang the police at two minutes after seven," Andrew told him.

"Dark at six?" Doona said. "In June?" As soon as she'd finished speaking, she held up a hand. "Other side of the world, isn't it? So, our summer is their winter, and vice versa. Just ignore me."

Andrew laughed. "Yes, our summer months are their winter months. So it was dark when Amelia got home. I'll let you read her statement in full, of course, but, basically, she arrived home and assumed her husband was out. When she went into the bedroom, she turned on the lights and saw him lying in bed. She immediately rang the police."

"How long had he been dead?" John asked.

"The post-mortem determined that he'd been dead for about twenty-four hours," Andrew replied.

"I'm surprised Amelia didn't notice any odd smells," Hugh remarked.

"The house was full of various air fresheners, the type that plug into outlets," Andrew told him. "They also had several of those spray bottles of fabric refreshers that make your clothes smell nice. It appeared that someone had sprayed the bed and the body with the contents of one of those bottles."

"So whoever killed him wanted to hide the smells for as long as possible," John mused.

"Maybe the killer wanted to make sure that Amelia didn't suspect anything until she actually stumbled across the body," Hugh said.

"Maybe, although Amelia wasn't expected back in Wellington until Friday afternoon. Due to certain circumstances, she changed her flight and returned home on Wednesday instead," Andrew replied.

"Certain circumstances?" Bessie repeated. "What circumstances?"

Andrew shook his head. "I'd rather you wait and read all of that in the file. I don't want anyone to have any preconceived notions about the suspects."

"So she didn't fly home early simply because she couldn't contact her husband," Doona said.

"She did not," Andrew agreed. "She came home, found the body, and called the police. There were plenty of suspects, but the case remains unsolved."

"How was he killed?" Harry asked.

"He was strangled," Andrew replied.

Bessie winced. *The crime scene photos are going to be grim,* she thought.

"It couldn't have been an accident?" Harry wondered.

Andrew shook his head. "No chance."

"Tell us about the suspects, then," John said.

"I'm going to give you a list of names, but I'm not going to tell you much about any of the people. You'll learn what you need to know when you read the case file," Andrew replied.

"Amelia has an alibi, though, right?" Bessie asked.

Andrew nodded. "She was in Auckland the day her husband was killed. The cities are only about an hour apart by plane, but Amelia was at a work conference, and she gave two of the presentations on the day in question. I will add that the police did everything they could to break her alibi, but they were unable to do so."

"So they thought she'd killed her husband," Hugh said thoughtfully. "Interesting."

"I'm not going to comment any further on that until you've read the file," Andrew replied. "Let's talk about the other suspects."

"Tell us about the dead man first," Bessie said. "You haven't told us anything besides his name."

"Sorry, I'm getting ahead of myself. Larry Irving was thirty-seven when he died. He was a nurse, working at a care home for the elderly near his home. I think that's enough about him for now. You'll discover more as you read the file."

Bessie nodded. "It's a start."

"Amelia was thirty-five when her husband died," Andrew added. "They'd been married for twelve years and had chosen not to have children. She worked for a pharmaceutical company. She and Larry met when she was on a sales call at the hospital where Larry worked before he changed jobs and went to work at the care home."

Bessie scribbled her notes as quickly as she could. Andrew always told her not to bother, as all of the information was in the file, but she preferred to have the basics in a neat list before she started reading what he gave them.

"You can find out more about Amelia's job and the company for which she worked in the file," Andrew said. "Let's talk about suspects. The police narrowed the list to five people. It's also possible that they were too quick to eliminate people from consideration, but we'll start with those five."

A loud ringing noise interrupted the conversation. Ken flushed and pulled out his mobile phone. He glanced at the screen and then shook his head.

"It can wait," he said, slipping the still-ringing device back into his pocket.

"Let me give you the names, and then we'll talk briefly about each person," Andrew said. "The suspects were Rosie Weber, James Irving, Eric Price, Oscar Manning, and Herbert Watts."

Bessie wrote them down, leaving space after each name for additional notes.

"Rosie was Larry's girlfriend," Andrew said after a moment.

"And the police are sure that Amelia didn't kill him?" Doona asked.

Andrew nodded. "They're certain of it."

"What can you tell us about Rosie?" Harry asked.

"She was twenty-nine at the time. She and Larry worked together. Rosie was also a nurse," Andrew replied.

"And that's all you're going to say about her," Doona guessed.

"For now. We'll talk about her in greater depth once you've all read the case file," Andrew said.

"James Irving was next," Harry said. "Was he related to the dead man?"

"He was Larry's younger brother," Andrew answered. "He

was thirty-two when his brother died. The two had had a falling-out about twelve years earlier and had only begun speaking to one another again a few weeks before Larry's death."

"What did they fall out about?" Charles asked.

Andrew hesitated. "Amelia," he said eventually. "You can read the details in the file, but James and Amelia had been involved briefly a few years before she met Larry. When she and Larry first started seeing one another, she didn't even realise that the two men were related."

"Interesting," John muttered as he made notes.

"What does James do for a living?" Doona asked.

"He works for one of the local banks," Andrew told her. "Or he did five years ago, anyway."

"Do we have updated information on what everyone is doing now?" Bessie asked.

"I have it, but I haven't given it to you," Andrew replied. He looked at Ken. "I usually give the team only the original case file at the start. When we meet again tomorrow, we'll talk about what was in the file, and then I'll give everyone any updates that are available. The next time we meet, we'll discuss those updates."

Ken nodded. "A lot can change in five years. It makes sense to start with the original file and then add the updates later."

"The next suspect is Eric Price," Andrew continued. "He was Amelia's immediate supervisor at the pharmaceutical company."

"And that makes him a suspect?" Hugh asked.

"There are reasons why he was a suspect," Andrew replied.

"Why wasn't he at the conference with Amelia?" Bessie wondered.

"He was at the conference, but, unlike Amelia, he was

unable to provide proof of where he was for the afternoon in question. He was supposed to be watching the sessions that Amelia presented, and he claims to have been in the audience for both, but no one else at the conference was prepared to swear that he was there," Andrew explained.

"So he could have flown back to Wellington, killed Larry, and then flown back to Auckland," Doona said. "That would have taken a lot of time and planning."

"And he would have been seen by a lot of people," Hugh suggested.

"Eric holds a private pilot's license," Andrew told them. "And he owns his own small plane. He flew himself and Amelia to the conference, and it's possible that he flew himself to Wellington and back again on the day that Larry died."

Bessie made another note and then frowned at her notebook. She hadn't read a word of the case file yet, but she was already disliking nearly everyone involved in the case.

"Oscar Manning was Larry's supervisor at the care home," Andrew continued. "He'd been in the job for only six months, and he'd already given Larry three written warnings about his behaviour."

"Was that typical for Larry?" Doona asked.

"In the nine and a half years that Larry had been there before Oscar arrived, he'd had a total of one written warning. I think it's safe to say that Larry and Oscar didn't get along well," Andrew replied.

"Did Oscar have any shared history with Amelia?" Hugh asked.

"There's nothing in the file to suggest that they'd ever met before Oscar had taken the job six months earlier. He actually relocated to Wellington from elsewhere in New Zealand when he was hired for the job, so it seems unlikely that he and Amelia had ever crossed paths prior to his arrival in the city," Andrew said.

"Who does that leave?" Doona asked. She glanced down at her notes. "Herbert Watts?"

"Herbert lived in the house next door to Amelia and Larry," Andrew told them. "They had frequent loud arguments about their shared fence."

"There you go," Harry said. "Herbert killed him." He dropped his pen and sat back in his chair. "I can't see why this wasn't solved five years ago."

A few people chuckled.

"Herbert had something approximating an alibi, in that he was supposed to be at work when Larry died," Andrew told them. "Unfortunately for Herbert, he couldn't prove that he'd been there. No one could prove that he hadn't been there, though, either."

"Where did he work?" Hugh asked.

"He worked for a small import and export business. His office was in a large building near the centre of Wellington, only a short distance from his home. At the time of the murder, Herbert was the company's only employee in Wellington, so he worked on his own in a tiny office space."

"So no one could confirm his alibi," Harry concluded.

"And there weren't any other suspects?" John asked.

Andrew shrugged. "Those were the ones identified immediately after the murder. Part of what we need to do is see if we can identify other people who are mentioned in the file who might be suspects. Of course, it could have been something completely random, but it didn't feel that way to the team that investigated the case. It doesn't feel that way to me, either."

"Was the front door locked when Amelia got home?" Doona asked.

Andrew nodded. "But the door had one of those locks that engage automatically when the door is shut."

"There must have been dozens and dozens of other suspects," John said. "What about patients or former patients? Maybe a patient passed away and the family blamed Larry for the death."

"The manager at the care home was insistent that not only had nothing like that ever happened to Larry, but that their employees' home addresses were carefully guarded secrets," Andrew replied. "It is something that was considered, but Inspector Harrison ruled it out."

"Inspector Harrison is your contact in Wellington?" John checked.

"He is. We've had several conversations about the case since the first time he reached out to me. He's quite young, and this was his first murder investigation. I know he's frustrated that it remains unsolved," Andrew said.

"And he thinks that something was missed," Doona said. "Otherwise he wouldn't have consulted you."

"He's willing to acknowledge that he may have missed something," Andrew agreed. "As I said, it was his first murder investigation. I think his biggest regret is the amount of time and effort that was spent trying to break Amelia's alibi. That time might have been better spent elsewhere."

"Anything else?" Harry asked.

Andrew looked down at his notes. "I don't think so, not at this point. We're meeting again tomorrow at the same time to talk about the initial investigation. Focus your efforts on finding gaps in the investigation. I'd like to go back to Inspector Harrison with a longer list of suspects than the list he gave me."

"That doesn't sound as if it will be difficult," Charles said.

Andrew nodded and then started handing out the large

envelopes that contained the case files. Bessie took hers and tucked it into her large handbag.

"I'll see you all tomorrow," Harry said as he headed for the door.

Charles was only a step or two behind him. "See you tomorrow," he called over his shoulder as he went.

"I assume they're eager to get started on the case," Ken said as the door shut behind the two men.

"They never stay to chat after the meetings," Doona told him. "They've both become friendlier over the last several months, but neither one of them is all that interested in small talk."

Ken nodded. "They're both very busy men, of course." He turned to Bessie. "I have a question for you. Did you know any of the others on the team before you found that body outside of your cottage?"

"Oh, yes, of course," Bessie replied. "I knew Hugh and Doona before I found the body. John had been on the island for only a short time before the murder, though, so I hadn't yet met him."

"Had you known Hugh and Doona for long?" Ken asked.

"I'd known Doona for about two years at that point," Bessie replied. "We'd met in a Manx language class."

"My marriage had just ended, and I thought it would be the perfect place to meet single men around my age," Doona told him. "As it happened, everyone in the class was much closer to Bessie's age than mine, and none of the students were single men, either."

"How old are you?" Ken asked Bessie.

She frowned at him. "I stopped counting when I got my free bus pass, and I don't plan to take any further notice of my age until I receive a card from the Queen," she told him.

Ken looked at Andrew, who slowly shook his head.

"I've never held a paying job – well, not before this one –

but if I had, I suppose I'd be retired by now," Bessie continued after a minute. "I consider myself to be towards the later part of middle age."

Ken raised an eyebrow and then nodded slowly. "So you met Doona in a Manx language class," he said. "And you became friends after that?"

Doona nodded. "In spite of the, um, slight difference in our ages, Bessie and I found that we had a lot in common as we struggled together to learn to speak an impossibly difficult language."

"And you knew Hugh as well?" Ken asked.

"Years ago, before she started getting caught up in so many murder investigations, Bessie used to act as something of an honorary auntie to the boys and girls of Laxey," Hugh explained. "We all grew up playing on Laxey Beach, which is her front garden. Most of us spent at least a night or two in her spare bedroom during our teen years. She was always sympathetic whenever any teen argued with his or her parents."

"I enjoyed being around children, and especially teenagers," Bessie added. "And most of them simply needed to get away for a day or two after a disagreement. I suspect many of them weren't actually all that upset with their parents. I always had cake and biscuits available. They might have been the key to my popularity."

Hugh laughed and then shook his head. "While most teens stayed with Bessie for only an odd night now and again, a few of us practically lived with her for years," he told Ken. "I was one of those kids. My parents wanted me to go to university, but I was determined to join the police right out of school. Bessie was sympathetic to both sides of the argument, and she let me stay with her for weeks at a time when I felt as if my parents were being impossible."

"How kind of her," Ken replied.

"It turns out my parents were right that I needed a university degree, though," Hugh said, shaking his head. "Bessie always told me that I'd never regret getting an education, but I was too stubborn to listen. I just hope that Grace and I do a better job with our kids than my parents did with me."

"I can see Aalish wanting to run away to Bessie's anyway," Doona said. "For cakes and biscuits, if nothing else."

Hugh laughed. "She's a lot like her father in that regard."

"Speaking of which, Jasper told me that we should take all of the biscuits when we go," Andrew said, nodding towards the table at the back of the room. "He was very apologetic that he hadn't been able to provide anything more exciting this time, but the hotel is incredibly busy with early summer guests."

"The biscuits were good," Ken said. "Much nicer than what we get at staff meetings at Scotland Yard."

"We get all sorts here," Hugh explained. "Sometimes the hotel's chef is trying out new recipes, so he makes us tiny portions of different potential menu items. A while back, they hired a new pastry chef, so we were given dozens of different fairy cakes and pastries to try."

"I knew I should have come last month," Ken said.

"We probably won't get much more than biscuits from now until the autumn," Andrew said. "Summer is the hotel's busiest time. We had some of our meetings in Laxey last month, but the beach cottages aren't really designed for business meetings."

"And I don't even have a beach cottage," Ken replied.

"That's next on my list of jobs," Andrew said. "I'm hoping Bessie can help."

CHAPTER 3

Bessie nodded. "I'm happy to help, but I'm not certain there is much I can do."

"Are there any hotels in Laxey?" Andrew asked.

"I believe there are a few rooms above the pub that may be available," Bessie replied. "I've no idea how busy they get, though. Otherwise, there's a small hotel in Lonan. I'm fairly certain they'll have vacancies. I doubt they ever have guests, actually."

"How do they stay in business, then?" Ken asked.

Bessie shrugged. "The hotel has been in the family for generations. It's small, and the owners have always had other businesses that pay their bills. I doubt the hotel does any better than breaking even each year. I don't think they actively try to attract guests, but I'm sure they're happy when they have some. It's probably been decades since they updated anything. You may well not want to stay there."

Ken frowned. "I don't know that I can afford to be particular at this point."

"You could always stay with Harry or Charles," Andrew suggested.

"If I absolutely have to, then I will, but I'd very much prefer my own space, and I'm sure they feel the same way," Ken replied.

"They have entire cottages to themselves, though," Bessie pointed out.

"Let's see what else we can find," Ken said. "I wish I could stay here. The Seaview is lovely."

"It's very nice," Bessie agreed. "Which is why it's so busy this time of year."

Bessie hugged her friends as they all got ready to leave the conference room.

"I'm going to hide in the library for an hour with my homework," Hugh told her. "Then I'm going to go home and play with Aalish for the rest of the day."

"Enjoy," she told him.

They all took the lift to the ground floor. Jasper Coventry was behind the reception desk as they strolled through the large foyer.

"Hello, Bessie," he said, rushing out from behind the desk to give her a hug.

"Hello," she replied.

"I hope your meeting went well," he said when he released her.

"It did," Andrew assured him. "And the biscuits were excellent."

Jasper nodded. "The new pastry chef is a bit overwhelmed now that every room in the hotel is booked and the restaurant is full at lunch and dinner every day. I didn't dare ask him for anything more complicated than plates of biscuits for you today."

"That's fine," Andrew replied. "We'll happily have the same again tomorrow."

"That's good, because that's probably exactly what you'll get," Jasper said.

"I don't suppose you've had any last-minute cancellations?" Andrew asked. "Ken needs a place to stay for the week, and the Seaview would be ideal."

Jasper shook his head. "Unfortunately, we are not only fully booked, but we're also overbooked. Someone, and I'm not going to mention any names, but someone who is no longer working for the Seaview, overbooked the entire month of June based on the misguided belief that at least ten per cent of our guests would cancel their bookings."

"Oh dear," Bessie said.

"Apparently, it's a common practice in London, where this person came from, but it isn't something I'm interested in doing here. We have far fewer options for relocating people if they arrive and we're overbooked. London is a huge city with thousands of hotels. This is a small island with a very limited number of hotels and guest houses."

"And the Seaview is the nicest hotel on the island. I imagine most people would be unhappy about being moved elsewhere if they were planning on staying here," Bessie said.

Jasper nodded. "It's been difficult. Fortunately, there have been a handful of cancellations, and we've been able to accommodate nearly everyone who has a booking, but we definitely don't have any rooms to spare. I am sorry."

"It's not your fault. Bringing Ken over was a last-minute decision on my part. We'll find somewhere for him to stay," Andrew replied. "We've three cottages on Laxey Beach, if nothing else."

"I can give you a list of some of the other hotels in Ramsey," Jasper said. "I suspect most of them are also fully booked, but you may find a room at one of them."

They walked together to the desk. Jasper went behind it and opened a drawer.

"It's a select list," he said as he passed a sheet of paper to

Andrew. "I've visited every hotel on the list myself, and they all met my standards, at least when I was there."

"As long as it's clean and not too noisy, I'm happy," Ken said. "I worked undercover for a few years, including several months of living on the streets. I'm not all that particular about hotel rooms now."

"These hotels were all clean when I visited them," Jasper replied. "How noisy they will be now will depend entirely on their current guests." He made a mark next to two of the names on the list. "Those are the two that I would expect to have the noisiest guests," he added.

"Thanks for this," Andrew said. He folded the sheet and stuck it in a pocket. "Shall we?"

The trio walked outside together.

"Most of the hotels are nearby, along this road," Andrew said. "Maybe we should just walk over and start knocking on doors, so to speak."

"It's a beautiful day for a stroll," Bessie said.

Ken nodded. "A bit of fresh air and sunshine will do me a world of good."

Half an hour later, they'd visited every hotel and guest house within walking distance.

"I suppose I could move from place to place each day," Ken said as they began to walk back towards the Seaview.

"If you did that, you'd have a place to stay tonight but not tomorrow night," Bessie said, looking at the notes she'd taken. "Then you'd have a place, or rather three different places, for the next three nights before you'd end up without anywhere for your last two nights on the island."

Andrew sighed. "Would you prefer to stay with Charles or Harry?" he asked.

Ken chuckled. "It might be best if I stayed with one for a few nights and then switched to the other. I don't want to overstay my welcome with either of them."

THE IRVING FILE

"I can ring the pub in Laxey and see if they have any rooms available," Bessie offered.

"Let's do that when we get back to my car," Andrew suggested.

A few minutes later, Bessie pulled out her mobile and rang directory enquiries. They gave her the number for the pub.

"Ah, yes, it's Bessie Cubbon," she said when someone picked up on the other end. "I was wondering if you had any rooms available?"

"No, we don't," the man snapped.

"Oh, that's a shame. I don't suppose you'll have any availability later in the week," she replied.

"No. We aren't renting rooms right now."

"Oh, I didn't realise that. Will you be renting them again in the near future?

"Hello?

"Hello? Is anyone there?"

Bessie frowned as her phone started beeping at her. "They seemed to think the conversation was over, even if I didn't," she told Andrew.

"They aren't renting rooms, then?" he asked.

She sighed and shook her head. "And the man wasn't very polite about it, either. I thought I knew just about everyone at the pub, but I don't believe he was anyone I know."

"Never mind. Where does that leave us?" Andrew asked.

"Didn't you mention somewhere in Lonan?" Ken asked. "I've no idea where Lonan is, but you did say you thought they'd have rooms available."

Bessie shook her head to get rid of the unsatisfactory conversation she'd just had and then nodded slowly. "Lonan is just a short distance from Laxey. If the hotel there is open, they should have rooms, but I suppose it's possible it's no longer in business. Maybe we should try ringing them before we drive over there."

"That might be wise," Andrew said.

Bessie rang directory enquiries again. Then she dialled the number she'd been given.

"The Margaret Hotel," a voice said.

"Ah, yes, I was wondering if you have any rooms available for this week," Bessie said.

"We do."

"Really? Excellent. My friend needs a room for seven nights. Can you accommodate him?"

"We can."

"Very good. We'll drive over now. We're just in Ramsey, so we'll be there soon."

"Fine."

Bessie couldn't think of anything to add, so she pushed the button to end the conversation. "Whoever that was, he wasn't very talkative," she told the others. "But they have a room for the week."

"Excellent," Ken said.

"Don't get too excited before you've seen it," Bessie warned him.

"As I said earlier, I'm not terribly particular. I really just need a bit of space to myself," Ken replied.

"Let's go and take a look," Andrew said. "Bessie, you'll have to navigate. Ken, you can follow me."

"Very good," Ken said.

Andrew waited until Ken was settled in the driver's seat of his hire car before he started his engine. Then he carefully drove out of the hotel's car park and headed back towards Laxey.

"Ken seems very nice," Bessie said after a moment.

Andrew laughed. "He's a good deal friendlier than the last person I brought to the island, anyway."

"I wasn't going to say that."

"You were too nice to say that. I know Nathan was difficult, but he's a solid inspector, and he's incredibly grateful to the team for the work that we did on the case he brought us."

"I'm glad we were able to help."

Andrew glanced at her. "He did suggest that maybe he should come across and thank the unit in person. I told him that that wasn't necessary."

"Completely unnecessary," Bessie quickly agreed.

Andrew chuckled. "Ken's here for a very different reason, though. The case we're considering isn't one of his, so he won't mind how much we question how the initial investigation was handled. Ken is just here to learn as much as he can about how the unit functions so that he can try to duplicate our success."

"I wish him luck. The more cold cases that can be solved, the better."

Andrew nodded. "Our case this month is interesting. I've read the file twice and, well, I'm getting ahead of myself. You should read the file before we have this conversation."

Bessie sighed. "Now I want to go home and start reading the file."

"I can take you home before Ken and I go to Lonan," Andrew offered. "You'll just have to give me directions to the hotel."

Bessie thought for a moment. "No, I'd rather go with you. It's been a great many years since I've been to The Margaret Hotel. I'm curious what's about been done to it since I was last there."

"The Margaret Hotel?"

"That's what it's called. It was named after the original owner's daughter, I believe. As I said earlier, it's been in the family for generations now. The current owner is Hilary Christian, and I do believe she's the last surviving member of the family. I'm not sure what will happen to the hotel when she dies."

"How old is she?"

Bessie thought for a moment. "She must be nearly seventy, or maybe even a bit past seventy. She had three brothers and one sister, and they were all very close in age. She's somewhere between sixty-five and seventy-five, anyway."

"And you said she's the last member of the family?"

"Of the immediate family, anyway. There may be some distant cousins somewhere on the island. The man who built the hotel was Donald Christian. He and his wife had two children, a son they called Duncan and their daughter, Margaret. They owned several properties in Lonan, and they built the hotel primarily to accommodate the men who used to come to the island to do business with Donald. After he died, Duncan took over, but he moved across after a few years and left his sister to run the businesses here."

"Across where?" Andrew asked.

Bessie shrugged. "I don't remember the details. Margaret stayed here, and from all accounts, did a good job running the businesses on the island. She never married, and she passed away more than thirty years ago. Duncan did get married. He and his wife had five children, the three boys and two girls that I mentioned earlier."

"And now only Hilary is left."

"That's right. Duncan and his wife moved back to the island after Margaret died. Their children were scattered around the world, but Hilary came to the island with them. She was unmarried, and even though she was over forty, Duncan and his wife thought it would be best if she stayed with them rather than living across on her own."

"What about the other children?"

Bessie frowned. "It's been a long time since I've thought

about any of these people. I'm trying to remember what happened to them all. I'm not certain I'm going to be able to remember every detail, but I feel quite certain that Hilary is the only one left in the family."

"Can you remember what happened to Duncan and his wife?"

"Duncan's wife passed away just a few months after they'd arrived on the island. I believe she told a few people that she thought she'd probably die of boredom not long after she arrived, but she actually caught a cold that turned into pneumonia. Duncan passed away about ten years later, leaving Hilary on her own to run what was left of the family businesses."

"And has she been as successful as her father and grandfather had been?"

"As far as I know, the companies are profitable," Bessie replied. "As I said earlier, I doubt the hotel makes any money, but I'm told the other businesses make up for it, and the family has always been inordinately fond of the hotel."

"Really?"

Bessie nodded. "Some years ago, back when Donald was still alive, the entire hotel burned to the ground. Donald insisted on rebuilding it. In my opinion, it was much nicer before they rebuilt it. Now it's a rather uninspiring rectangular block of the sort that was oddly popular in the sixties."

"And you don't remember what happened to any of Duncan's other children?" Andrew asked. "Am I just continuing on from here?" he added before Bessie could reply.

"Yes, just follow this road through Laxey. Eventually, we'll reach Lonan," she told him. "As for the other children, I believe Hilary's sister, Harriet, died when she was very young – under ten, anyway. She may have been born with some life-limiting genetic condition, but I may be confusing her with someone else. Regardless, I'm quite certain she died when she was young."

"And the three boys?"

"Harold, Harvey, and Henry," Bessie recalled. "I do remember hearing about Harold. He studied religion at university and then decided to become a Catholic priest. I believe he may have even joined some sort of monastic community or some such thing. I remember talking with Hilary about it once. She laughed about her brother, the priest, living alone on a mountain in Spain or something similar."

"I wasn't expecting that," Andrew admitted.

"Harvey was a keen cricketer. It's all coming back to me now. Hilary and I had lunch together one afternoon about twenty years ago. It was a charity event, and we were the only single women there, so they put us at a table together. I was quite used to such things, but Hilary wasn't very involved in the island's charities, so she felt a bit out of her depth there."

"So you talked to her all afternoon," Andrew guessed.

"I did, and then I met her for lunch the following week and we talked some more. We actually met for lunch about once a month for the next few months, but then she got busy with something, or perhaps I did, and we fell out of the habit. I'm almost ashamed to say that I haven't seen her since, except in passing."

"What else can you tell me about Harvey?"

"As I said, he was a keen cricketer. He wanted to play professionally, but he wasn't quite good enough. After university, he spent a few years playing for some small teams in different places before taking a position as an assistant coach for some team somewhere near Dover, although I may not be remembering that correctly. Sadly, he was killed in a car accident when he was in his early thirties.

If I'm remembering correctly, he was engaged to be married at the time."

"How sad."

Bessie smiled. "Hilary admitted to me that she wasn't fond of the woman he was planning to marry. She felt vindicated when the woman in question married someone else only four months after Harvey's death."

"That's very quick."

"Indeed."

"And that leaves only one brother."

"Henry," Bessie said. "He was the baby of the family, and Hilary always felt as if he was their mother's favourite. Hilary told me that he was quite spoiled and selfish and that they weren't close as children."

"Do you know what happened to him?"

Bessie shrugged. "I seem to recall that he got involved with the wrong crowd at university and ended up addicted to something horrible. Sadly, I believe he died of a drug overdose not long after."

"How awful."

"And now Hilary is the only one left," Bessie said. "I'm not sure how many of the family businesses she still owns. I suspect she's sold most of them off over the years. She may even have sold the hotel."

"At least they have rooms available. That's all that matters to me."

Bessie laughed. "Let's see what sort of condition the rooms are in before you get too excited. You need to turn left here."

Andrew turned down the narrow road that led to the hotel. After a blind curve, the road ended in a small car park next to the unattractive, blocky building that was The Margaret Hotel.

"It's, um, well…" Andrew said as he parked the car.

"Exactly," Bessie said. "Let's hope it's slightly nicer on the inside," she added before she got out of the car.

Ken parked next to Andrew and slowly climbed out of his car. "You did warn me," he said to Bessie as the three of them walked towards the building.

"I assume we want that door," Andrew said, pointing to the door with the "Office" sign stuck on it.

The other doors were numbered from one to six. Bessie looked at the stuck-on numbers, none of which matched, and sighed. Most of them were crooked, some were faded, and others appeared to be sliding down the doors, leaving a trail of sticky glue behind them.

"Maybe you should just stay with Harry," Andrew suggested.

Ken shook his head. "We're here now. I may as well at least see a room."

Bessie walked over to the office door and knocked loudly. When the door swung open, she smiled at the man who'd opened it. He looked to be somewhere in his fifties, with tangled grey hair and bloodshot brown eyes. He smelled of cigarette smoke and beer.

"Good afternoon," she said. "I rang earlier. My friend needs a place to stay for seven nights."

He stared at her for a moment and then looked past her at the two men behind her. Without speaking, he turned and walked back into the office. Bessie glanced at the others and then shrugged and followed him inside.

The room was mostly empty, with only a small desk and chair in one corner and a rocking chair in front of the electric fireplace. The woman rocking in the chair looked up as Bessie entered.

"Elizabeth Cubbon? I don't believe it. What brings you here?" she asked.

"Hilary?" Bessie replied. "It's good to see you again. I have a friend visiting the island. He needs a place to stay for a week."

"And you brought him here? I know the island is busy this time of year, but I didn't expect you to be that desperate." Hilary replied, laughing loudly at her words.

Bessie grinned. "We are that desperate," she admitted.

"Well, I'm sure we have a room. We have five, actually, because Harlan here is staying in Room 1. But you haven't met Harlan yet. This is my nephew, Harlan Christian. Harlan, this is Bessie Cubbon."

The man looked up from behind the desk and nodded at Bessie.

"Your nephew?" Bessie repeated questioningly.

Hilary grinned. "He's Harold's son," she told her.

CHAPTER 4

Bessie stared at Hilary. "Harold's son?" she repeated. "How is that even possible? He was a priest, wasn't he?"

Hilary laughed. "As if he'd be the first priest to have ever had a child," she said. "Wasn't priestly corruption one of the reasons why we had a Reformation? Oh, I know, it was mostly about Henry the Eighth wanting a new young wife who could give him boys, but where was I? Oh, yes, Harlan. Harold decided to become a priest after he finished uni. I never once imagined that he was a saint during his uni days."

Bessie looked at Harlan. He certainly appeared old enough to have been conceived while Harold was still at university. "When did you find out about him?" she asked.

"I should let Harlan tell you the story," Hilary replied. She looked over at the man, who was standing still, staring into space. "Do you want to tell it?" she asked.

He looked at her and shrugged. "You tell."

Hilary nodded and then settled back in her chair. "I got a letter about six months ago from Harlan. His mother had just passed away and he'd been going through her things. She never named a father on Harlan's birth certificate, but he found some letters in one of her boxes of papers, letters that she'd written but never sent."

"Letters that she'd written but never sent? What does that mean?" Bessie asked.

"Harlan's mother, Cassandra, never told Harold about Harlan," Hilary explained. "Harlan found a half-dozen or so letters, written over many years. She kept writing them, telling my brother that he was a father, but she never actually sent any of them."

Bessie frowned. "Why not?"

"In the first one, she'd only just learned that she was pregnant. She's apologetic, as if falling pregnant was entirely her fault, and she says she hopes the news won't ruin Harold's life. In the second one, she says she never sent the first because she'd decided to wait in case anything went wrong. In the third, she talks about not sending the second because she'd heard that Harold was considering becoming a priest and she didn't want to influence his decision. There are another three or four letters, and each one starts with an explanation of why the previous one was never sent," Hilary explained. "In the end, she left the letters for Harlan to find."

"You must have been surprised," Bessie said to Harlan.

He shrugged. "Some."

"She'd always told Harlan that he was the result of a one-night stand, but the letters tell a very different story," Hilary continued. "From what I read, Harold and Cassandra were very much in love, but they were both very young and the relationship simply didn't last. Of course, if Harold had known about the baby, he would have insisted on marrying Cassandra."

Ken cleared his throat. "Have you considered DNA testing?" he asked.

Hilary stared at him. "I read the letters myself," she said.

Ken nodded. "DNA testing can still be a good idea. You never met Cassandra. You've no idea if she was being entirely truthful in her letters."

"Was your mum a liar?" Hilary asked Harlan.

He shook his head.

"There you go," Hilary said flatly.

Ken opened his mouth and then closed it again.

"Congratulations on acquiring a nephew, then," Bessie said after an awkward pause.

"Thank you," Hilary replied. "It's been a long time since I've had family around. It's nice to have Harlan here."

"Where were you before you came to the island?" Andrew asked the man.

"London," Harlan replied.

"Where in London? It's a big city," Andrew said with a grin.

"I moved a lot," was the unsatisfactory reply.

"Did you say you wanted a room?" Hilary asked.

"Yes, please, for seven nights," Ken told her.

"Harlan, give him the key to Room 6," Hilary said. "And run his credit card through the machine."

Ken handed Harlan his credit card and then looked over at Hilary. "I'm afraid to ask how much you're going to charge me. Every other hotel on the island seems to be fully booked."

Hilary shrugged. "My rates don't change. It's fifty pounds a night for the room. That doesn't include breakfast, but I'm here every morning at eight, and the first thing I always do is make a pot of coffee. If you get here before I drink it all, you can have a cup."

"I'll keep that in mind," Ken replied.

"There aren't any coffee-making facilities in the room?" Andrew asked.

"They're a fire hazard," Hilary told him. "No hair dryers, either."

Harlan had been digging through a drawer during the conversation. Now he pulled out a key attached to a large plastic disc. As he passed the key to Ken, Bessie noticed that the disc said, "If Found, Please Return to The Babbingstone Hotel, Liverpool." A small piece of tape with the number six on it had been stuck across the bottom of the circle.

"We'll be here if you need anything," Hilary said as Ken took the key.

"Thanks," Ken replied.

Feeling as if they'd been dismissed, Bessie said a quick goodbye to Hilary and Harlan and then turned and followed the two men out of the room. Room 6 was as far away from the office as it was possible to be. Ken pushed the key into the lock and then tried to turn it.

"It may not get used very often," Andrew said.

Ken jiggled the key a few times. Eventually, it turned. As he pushed on the door, the hinges squealed loudly. He pushed it open and then switched on the light.

"It's fine," he said quickly as the dim bulb struggled to illuminate the small room.

"It smells musty," Bessie said.

"There probably hasn't been anyone in here in years," Ken replied as he walked into the room.

"You should ask for fresh bedding," Andrew suggested.

Ken shook his head. "This is fine. I'm really not all that particular."

Bessie frowned. "Check that you have running water," she said.

"And hot water," Andrew added.

Ken walked into the adjoining bathroom. There were squeaks and groans from the plumbing, but after a moment,

Bessie could hear water running. Then she heard the loo flush, too. When Ken emerged, he smiled at them.

"Everything seems to be working and the water gets quite nice and hot. I'm sure I'll be fine here," he said.

"It's pretty dark in here," Bessie pointed out.

"I have a little book light that someone gave me for Christmas one year. It's bright enough to read by, so I can get started on the case file," Ken told her.

"Do you want to meet for dinner somewhere?" Andrew asked.

"We could. I don't want to be a bother, though," Ken replied.

"It's no bother," Andrew said. "Can you find your way back to Laxey? We drove past it on the way here."

"I remember, and I'm sure I can find it again."

Andrew gave Ken directions to one of Bessie's favorite Laxey restaurants.

"We'll see you there at six," Andrew said as he and Bessie left the room.

"Sounds good," Ken replied. "Thanks for finding me a place to stay," he told Bessie.

"I wish I could have found you something a bit nicer," she replied. It wasn't until she and Andrew were on their way back to Laxey that she spoke again.

"I'm not certain what to think of Harlan," she said. "Hilary seemed happy to believe his story, but I found it all a bit odd."

Andrew nodded. "I'm going to ring a friend of mine and see if someone can make some discreet enquiries about the man. He may be exactly who he claims to be, or he may be trying to scam Hilary."

"I'm not certain how much Hilary is worth now."

"You did say she was the last surviving member of her family. I wonder who will inherit the hotel and anything else she owns."

"That's a good question. The hotel probably isn't worth much, but property prices on the island have been rising so quickly, that it could be worth quite a bit more than I suspect. If nothing else, the land it's on must have value."

"Hilary was adamant that she didn't want to have any DNA tests done."

"I wonder why. If I were her, I'd want to be absolutely certain about the man's parentage."

They chatted about families and DNA tests for the rest of the short drive back to Bessie's cottage.

"Now, do you want to spend some time with the case file, or would you rather spend some time with Helen?" Andrew asked as he parked his car in the parking area outside of Bessie's cottage.

"What an impossible choice," Bessie replied with a laugh. "I'd love to spend some time with Helen, but I really ought to start reading the case file."

"It isn't all that long until dinner, though. You'd barely have time to get started on the case file."

"Anyone would think that you don't want me to do my work," Bessie protested.

"I just don't want to be alone with Helen," Andrew admitted. "We had something of a disagreement this morning, and I'm not eager to pick up the conversation where we left it."

Bessie frowned at him. "It sounds very much as if that's exactly what you should do. You go and talk to Helen. I'll read the first few pages of the case file, and then we can all have a lovely dinner together."

Andrew sighed. "You're right, of course. I'll go and talk to Helen. We'll need to leave around ten to six for dinner."

"I'll meet you here, at your car," Bessie said before opening her door and climbing out. "Good luck," she added.

"Thanks, but Helen is usually very reasonable, really. I'm fairly certain the conversation won't be too painful."

Bessie let herself into her cottage and looked at the clock. She had not much more than an hour to get started on the case file. After switching on the kettle, she sat down at the table and opened her envelope. When the kettle boiled, she decided that she didn't need tea. She was too engrossed in the case to bother. A knock on her door interrupted her.

"Andrew?" she said as she opened the door. She looked at the clock and flushed. "I am so sorry," she said as she realised the time. "I lost all track of time."

He smiled at her. "It's not a problem, but we do need to get to the restaurant if we're going to meet Ken."

"Give me two minutes," Bessie said. She gathered up the papers that she had spread all over the kitchen table, quickly shoving them back into their envelope. Then she took the envelope up to her office and locked it in a desk drawer. After running a comb through her hair and powdering her nose, she was ready to go.

Helen was standing with her father at his car when Bessie emerged from her cottage. The two women greeted one another with a hug.

"It's lovely to see you again," Bessie told the younger woman. "I'm so glad you found time to come with your father again this month."

"I'm not sure I'm going to be able to keep doing this forever, but it's a lovely break for me, too," Helen replied. "I'm looking forward to seeing more of your beautiful island and also to having some long and incredibly lazy days in the cottage, curled up with a good book. I brought six."

Bessie laughed. "That should be enough to see you through a fortnight."

"I hope so, although Dad did promise me a trip to the bookshop in Ramsey one day."

"It's a wonderful shop, and I never get out of there without spending far too much. If you do need more reading material, though, you are more than welcome to borrow some books from me. I have two entire bookshelves full of books that are specifically for lending."

"I may take you up on that."

The drive to the restaurant didn't take long. As Andrew parked the car, Bessie spotted Ken, who was sitting in his hire car a few spaces away.

"I hope you haven't been waiting long," Bessie told him as he emerged from his car. "I'm afraid it's my fault that we're late. I'm very sorry, but I got quite lost in the case file and forgot all about dinner."

"It's not a problem. I only just arrived myself. And now I'm glad that I didn't open the case file before I met you. I was afraid the same thing might happen to me," Ken replied.

They walked into the restaurant and were shown to a table in a dark corner.

"I'll never be able to read the menu back here," Helen said, angling her menu in different directions to try to shed more light on it.

"Use this," Andrew suggested, handing her a small torch.

"I shall feel quite ridiculous doing so, but I don't think I have much choice," Helen replied.

"I'm just going to wait and see what the specials are," Bessie told her. "I'm sure something there will sound good, and then I don't have to read the menu."

"That's an excellent idea," Ken said, putting his menu down on the table.

The waiter arrived a moment later, and once he'd listed all of the day's specials, everyone decided to order from that list. Helen handed her father the torch as she settled back in her seat.

"What shall we talk about?" she asked as she looked from Bessie to Ken and back again.

"We can't talk about the case," Andrew reminded them.

"As I haven't even opened the file, that's a good thing," Ken laughed.

"How is your room?" Bessie asked.

Ken shrugged. "The chair is quite hard and lumpy, but it's a place to sit down. The lamp on the desk is actually quite bright, so I should be able to read my case file once I find time to actually do so. I haven't tried the bed yet, but I assume the mattress will be either too hard or too soft, and probably quite lumpy as well, but regardless, it's a clean, warm, dry, safe place to sleep, so I won't complain."

"Most people would," Helen told him.

"And if I did, what good would it do?" Ken asked. "No amount of complaining will suddenly conjure up a room elsewhere. The Margaret Hotel is the only one on the island that has availability right now, so I need to make the best of it."

"There may be a few places in the south of the island with rooms," Bessie said thoughtfully.

Ken shook his head. "I know it's a fairly small island, but I'd much rather stay where I am and be close to The Seaview and Laxey than move to the south. I'll be absolutely fine at The Margaret, I promise."

"What did you think of Hilary's newly discovered nephew?" Bessie asked.

Ken frowned. "If I were at home, I'd probably ring a few people and see if I could learn anything more about the man."

"I'm already working on that," Andrew assured him. "I told Helen the story when I got back to my cottage," he added.

"And I thought the entire thing sounded incredibly suspicious," Helen said. "I suspect that man, whoever he actually is, is just trying to get his hands on Hilary's money."

"I don't know that she has much money," Bessie replied. "She might have sold all of the family businesses years ago."

"I suspect she has a good deal more than her supposed nephew, anyway," Helen countered.

"You're probably right about that," Bessie said with a sigh.

"I'm going to make a few discreet enquiries," Andrew told them. "I don't want to upset Hilary, but I am curious about the man."

"Do you need his fingerprints?" Helen asked. "I've always wanted to try to get someone's fingerprints. I could go and ask about a room, but I'm not sure what I could try to get him to touch."

"I don't think we need to go that far – not yet, anyway," Andrew replied.

"I had to get someone's fingerprints once," Bessie said. "I invited the man for tea and then gave him lemonade."

"You can't stop there," Helen said as Bessie took a sip of her drink. "Did you manage to get usable prints? Was the man someone other than who he claimed to be? Did he go to prison?"

Bessie laughed. "Yes, yes, and yes."

Helen insisted on hearing the entire story, which Bessie only just finished as the food arrived.

"I don't suppose you've any reason to invite this Harlan Christian to your house for tea," Helen said as the waiter walked away. "Maybe you could take an envelope to the hotel and tell them that it's for Ken. You could ask Harlan to deliver it to Ken's room."

"It's far too soon to be worrying about getting the man's fingerprints," Andrew said. "Let me see what I can learn about him from my sources first."

"Maybe I could drop off cookies for Ken," Helen said thoughtfully. "I could put them in a plastic container. Would that work for fingerprints?"

"The weather seems very pleasant for this time of year," Andrew said.

Helen made a face at him. "He doesn't want me involved," she told Bessie.

"I just think it's too soon to be worrying about fingerprints. I promise, if we do end up needing some, that I'll let you be a part of the job, okay?" he asked her.

Helen beamed. "Thanks, Dad."

"And now, let's talk about other, more pleasant topics," Andrew suggested.

The foursome chatted about the weather and some of the island's historical sites as they ate. Over pudding, Bessie, Andrew, and Helen made tentative plans to do some sightseeing together during the following week.

"For now, we need to focus on the case, of course," Andrew said as the waiter handed him the bill. "But we should have some time to sightsee next week, assuming things are going well."

"We always have days in between meetings when we're simply waiting for replies," Bessie said. "Those are good days for sightseeing, because otherwise we just sit around and get frustrated."

Ken grinned. "I should be taking notes. I don't want my team sitting around getting frustrated."

"What are your plans for the rest of the evening?" Andrew asked Ken as they walked back to their cars.

"I'm going back to start reading through the case file. I'd like to read everything once and then get some sleep. I'm hoping inspiration will strike overnight."

"At this point, the goal is to find gaps in the initial investigation, things we think were missed, or questions that we want the witnesses asked," Andrew told him.

"And here I was, hoping to solve the entire case by morning," Ken replied.

"That would be a bonus," Bessie said. "We could do a lot more sightseeing together."

Ken laughed. "I suppose I'd better get started, then."

He climbed into his car and drove away as Bessie and the others got into Andrew's car.

CHAPTER 5

"And now, my books are calling to me," Helen said as Andrew parked just outside of Bessie's cottage. "I may see you in the morning," she told Bessie. "If I'm up, I'd love to join you for a walk."

"You know I'll be walking," Bessie replied. She credited a great deal of her continued good health to her practice of walking on the beach every morning. While she enjoyed walking alone, she was also generally happy to have company while she strolled.

"Would you like to come in for a cuppa?" Bessie asked Andrew as they all emerged from the car.

"I would love to," he replied.

Helen headed towards the first of the row of holiday cottages that stretched along the beach just beyond Bessie's own small cottage. Andrew had been using that cottage as his home for his fortnights on the island since the very first meetings of the cold case unit. Bessie and Andrew turned in the opposite direction and walked the short distance to Bessie's door.

"Have you read enough of the case file to start talking

about the case?" Andrew asked as Bessie switched the kettle on.

"I suppose so, although I still have a long way to go."

"How much have you read?"

"I read everyone's initial statements," Bessie replied. "And it was all quite sad, really."

"Sad?"

"I felt very sorry for Amelia, coming home from her trip, and finding her husband dead in their bed. I could almost feel her shock and horror when I read the transcript from her conversation with the emergency department."

"She was clearly horrified," Andrew agreed.

"And then I read her initial statement, during which she talked repeatedly about how much she'd loved her husband, right up until she started talking about her boyfriend."

Andrew sighed. "They did have a rather complicated relationship."

Bessie piled biscuits onto a plate and put it at the centre of the table. After adding small plates for each of them, she made the tea. Andrew was nibbling on a biscuit as she put the teacups down and joined him at the table.

"'Complicated' is one way of describing it. And it sounds as if it would have become a lot more complicated if Larry hadn't died when he did."

Andrew nodded. "Amelia was certain that Larry didn't know that she was involved with her supervisor, Eric Price."

"According to her interview, and his, for that matter, they were incredibly discreet."

"Right up until his wife, Janice, found out, anyway."

Bessie frowned. "How did Janice find out?"

"That's a very good question, one that I don't think Janice ever answered. It's already on my list of things for Inspector Harrison to ask her when he talks to her again."

"Eric said that he had no idea how his wife had found

out," Bessie recalled. "But once she did, it was only going to be a matter of time before Larry found out as well."

"Janice is the reason why Amelia flew home early from the conference. Janice insisted that she had to go, and Eric was very quick to agree."

"Which made Amelia furious, but, from what she said, her job was at stake if she didn't agree. I have to say, though, that I would have thought her job was at stake anyway. Surely Janice wasn't going to let Amelia keep working with Eric?"

"I'm not certain that Janice could have forced Eric to let her go."

"Maybe not, but she certainly could have forced Eric to find another job," Bessie argued. "If I found out that my husband was having an affair with a work colleague, I'd make him find another job immediately."

"And you'll find out tomorrow if Janice made Eric find a new job."

Bessie frowned. "You already know, don't you?"

"Actually, I haven't read the updates myself yet. I want all of us to be on the same page tomorrow, when we have our first meeting about the case."

"Amelia said she hadn't been looking forward to telling Larry about her affair, but she also said that she and Eric were in love and that they wanted to be together."

Andrew nodded. "Eric told a slightly different story."

"When the police first questioned him, they didn't tell him that Larry was dead. He seemed to assume that they wanted to talk to him about the scene that Janice had caused at the conference."

"From the sound of it, it was quite the scene."

"Where was Janice when Larry was killed?"

Andrew looked surprised. "I'm not sure that she had a motive for killing him."

"I don't know that she did, but she was clearly very angry.

Maybe Larry was the one who told her about the affair, and she was so upset that she killed him."

"From all accounts, Janice barely knew the man. Besides, as soon as she found out about the affair, she caught the next available flight to Auckland. I don't know that she would have had time to kill Larry on her way to the airport."

"Or so she claimed. What if she'd found out about the affair days or even weeks earlier and was just waiting for the right time to get her revenge? Maybe she killed Larry and then drove to the airport for the confrontation after weeks of planning."

Andrew shrugged. "I read the police reports from when the hotel rang them while Janice was still shouting and throwing things, long before Larry's body was found. Janice's actions were very much what I would have expected from a woman who'd just found out that her husband was cheating."

"She walked into the keynote speech and stood at the back of the room and waited until the speaker finished," Bessie said. "She wasn't supposed to be there, though. Eric had left her back in Wellington with their children."

"Which could mean that she had the opportunity to murder Larry," Andrew admitted.

"She said in her statement that someone rang her and told her that Eric was at the conference with his lover, Amelia, and that if she was smart, she'd go and confront them."

"And she claimed that she didn't recognise the voice."

"But she trusted this random stranger enough to take the children to her mother's house and then fly to Auckland to confront her husband."

"Yeah, I suspect she knew the identity of the person who rang."

"I do as well."

"So she flew to Auckland and then walked into the

keynote speech. As the speaker finished, Eric rushed to the back of the room to find out why she was there."

"Just as people were lining up at the back of the room to ask questions of the speaker," Bessie said. "Which meant there was a microphone right next to Janice."

Andrew chuckled. "From what I read, I don't know that she needed a microphone. Nearly all of the witnesses said that she was shouting quite loudly."

"I don't blame her one bit."

"Nor do I, of course. It was unfortunate that when she started shouting, Amelia rushed over to try to calm her down."

"Yes, I found it quite sad that Janice and Amelia were friends, or at least Janice thought they were friends."

"Basically, the entire conference got to hear Janice accuse Eric and Amelia of having an affair and then got to listen as Eric tried to deny it."

"From what the witnesses said, he could barely manage to string words together into sentences, and there wasn't a person in the room who believed anything he said."

Andrew nodded. "Although from what I read, no one there had ever suspected that the pair were involved, not until that afternoon."

Bessie sighed. "After Eric's passionate, if badly worded and unconvincing denials, Amelia stepped in and just admitted to everything. She told Janice that she and Eric were in love and that she was sorry, but that they wanted to be together."

"And that's when Janice started throwing things," Andrew said.

"At least she limited herself to the biscuits on the table near the door and didn't actually throw any furniture."

"And then hotel security stepped in, and the police

arrived. Eric told Amelia to go home and try to save her marriage while he did what he could to rescue his."

"Which made Amelia furious, of course. She asked Eric to run away with her, but he just kept insisting that she had to go home immediately. Eventually, the police and the owners of the company for which they both worked stepped in and insisted that Amelia should leave. So she flew home, angry and upset, and then found her husband's body in their bedroom," Bessie concluded.

Andrew nodded. "So you have both Eric and Janice on your list of suspects?"

"Yes, although I'm not certain of a motive for either of them, really. Maybe Larry had found out about the affair and Eric was afraid that he'd tell Janice."

"I suppose that's one possibility."

"Of course, it's also possible that he simply wanted to eliminate Larry," Bessie said thoughtfully. "Maybe he really did think that he wanted to be with Amelia, and he was prepared to get rid of Larry to make that happen. Maybe he was only telling Janice what he thought she wanted to hear in the immediate aftermath of the big scene in Auckland."

"It will be interesting to find out where everyone is now," Andrew said. "Why might Janice have killed him?"

"Maybe, once she found out about the affair, she felt as if Eric were dead to her, and she wanted Amelia to suffer in the same way."

"That's actually very good," Andrew said. "Except it would mean that Janice found out about the affair the day before she flew to Auckland. Do you think she would have waited a full day before flying out to confront Eric?"

"Maybe the flights were all full on the day she found out. Maybe she needed to find someone to watch the kids. Maybe she'd known about the affair for weeks and was simply biding her time."

"All of which suggests that she must be an amazing actress."

"I know I say this with every case, but I really wish I could meet everyone this time around."

Andrew nodded. "I know what you mean. I was fascinated by everything I read about Janice. I'd really like to meet her."

"Maybe the next unit meeting should take place in New Zealand," Bessie suggested. "The change of scenery might be good for all of us."

"I don't think our budget would stretch to a trip halfway around the world, but I do share your frustration."

"I don't know that we can talk productively any further about Eric or Janice, not until we know where they both are now."

"But that still leaves a number of other suspects," Andrew said.

"Yes, like Larry's girlfriend, Rosie."

"It may just be because of the contrast between her and Janice and Amelia, but to me she seemed oddly unemotional about the murder of her lover," Andrew said.

"I felt that, too. The police questioned her about her whereabouts on the day that Larry died before they told her that he was dead. When they first started asking, they reported that she seemed amused."

"She said something along the lines of 'someone's found out about me and Larry, huh? I don't think it's a police matter, though,'" Andrew said.

"According to her statement, given before she knew he was dead, she and Larry had been seeing one another for about two years, but it was just casual."

"Basically, they were simply sleeping together whenever the opportunity arose."

"But she denied having seen him on the day he died,"

Bessie said. "He'd taken a few days off from work, mostly because he was angry with Oscar for all of the written warnings, but she told the police that they hadn't made plans to get together, even though they nearly always did so when Amelia was out of town."

"She doesn't have an alibi for the time when Larry died," Andrew said. "The question is, did she have a motive?"

"Maybe she was lying about her feelings for the man. Maybe she was madly in love with him, but he was just having fun."

"That's one possibility."

"When she was told that Amelia had come back from her conference early because she'd been caught having an affair with her supervisor, the police reported that Rosie laughed for a really long time."

"And said something about how much time and energy Larry had wasted on feeling guilty," Bessie recalled. "I can't wait to see where she is now."

"Anything else about her, or should we move on?" Andrew asked.

"Let's move on. It's getting late," Bessie said, glancing at the clock. "James Irving, the victim's brother, had some interesting things to say."

"He did indeed."

"I felt quite sorry for him, really. He told the police that Amelia was the love of his life and that he didn't think he'd ever get over losing her."

"At least he and his brother were working on reconciling before Larry died," Andrew said.

"James wasn't very clear on why they'd started talking again, though. He just said that one of them had finally rung the other and suggested a meeting. I'd like to know which of them suggested the meeting and what was said the first time they spoke after over ten years of estrangement."

"He did admit that he couldn't really blame his brother for what had happened. I'm trying to remember the whole story, but I may have bits of it wrong. He and Amelia met when he was just eighteen. She was a few years older."

Bessie nodded. "They'd met at a party thrown by a mutual friend, and, according to James, it was love at first sight."

"Amelia sort of agreed with him when she was questioned about the relationship. It may be just me, but I got the impression that she hadn't been nearly as much in love as James was, though."

"Clearly she hadn't, because she ended things with him just a few months later."

"And from all accounts, they didn't see one another again until Larry brought Amelia to dinner with James one night."

"And as soon as James saw her and found out that she was involved with Larry, he walked out of the restaurant and didn't speak to his brother again for the next twelve years," Bessie concluded.

"Amelia said that Larry had invited James to their wedding, but James claimed he'd never received an invitation, something that made him angry, even though he also said that he wouldn't have gone, even if he had been invited."

"If I were Larry, I don't think I would have invited James. I would have worried that he might object in the middle of the ceremony."

"But they were working on rebuilding their relationship in the weeks before Larry's death," Andrew said. "Or so James claimed."

"If James were angry enough about Larry's relationship with Amelia to kill him over it, why would he wait twelve years?" Bessie asked.

"Why did he wait twelve years to talk to him again?"

Bessie sighed. "The police need to talk to James again. We have a lot of questions for him."

"He didn't have an alibi for the night that his brother died."

"He said he was at home alone, but there was no way he could prove that. I do hope he isn't involved with Amelia now."

"Why?"

Bessie shrugged. "I suppose mostly because if they are involved now, it will make it seem more likely that James killed his brother. And if he did, well, that's just terribly sad."

"The fact that Larry was murdered is terribly sad."

"Yes, of course. I don't suppose there's any way the police got it wrong, and he simply had a heart attack or something."

"You saw the crime scene photos."

Bessie shivered. "I did. And I read the autopsy report, although I really just skimmed it. I'll probably go back and read it more carefully later, but I will admit that I'm hoping I don't need to."

"It basically says that he was strangled by the belt that was around his neck," Andrew told her.

"How awful for him."

"He'd been drinking and may well have been passed out when the killer struck. There was no sign that he tried to fight against his attacker, anyway."

Bessie sighed. "Sometimes I think we live in a horrible world."

"Which is why I do what I do."

"But we were talking about James. He doesn't have an alibi. Did he have a motive?"

"I think we need to find out what had recently changed before we can answer that. He and Larry were talking again. Why? Is it possible that James learned something about Larry's marriage that upset him so much that he killed Larry?"

"Maybe he found out that Larry was having an affair,"

Bessie suggested.

"Or maybe he found out that Amelia was, and he blamed his brother for not making her happy," Andrew replied. "Either is possible."

"I don't suppose you'll let me read any of the updates tonight."

Andrew chuckled. "I'm very tempted to say yes, just so I can read them, too, but that wouldn't be fair to the rest of the unit. I really do think it's best if we talk about the case first without knowing where everyone is now, though. I know it's annoying, but I think we get better results when we do it my way."

"Maybe Ken can run his unit differently and then we can compare results," Bessie said. "Maybe his unit will be just as successful even if they do read everything all at once."

"Maybe, but for now we're doing unbelievably well. I'd rather not change anything, not when we're putting murderers behind bars every single month."

Bessie nodded. "Who else is on the suspect list?"

"Oscar Manning."

"Oh, him," Bessie replied flatly. "I'd love to think that he did it, because he seemed like a thoroughly disagreeable person, but I can't imagine him caring enough about anyone or anything to actually commit a murder."

Andrew chuckled. "I take it you didn't care for Mr. Manning?"

"He was quite horrible, and you know it. From what was said in the interview, I got the impression that he kept giving Larry written warnings whenever Larry did anything remotely helpful for a patient."

"Helpful, but, strictly speaking, against the rules."

"I hope I won't have to go and live in a care home when I get old, but if I do, I want a nurse like Larry, and I hope he won't have a supervisor like Oscar."

THE IRVING FILE

Andrew nodded. "Larry came across as caring and compassionate, willing to bend the rules a bit to make his patients more comfortable."

"And Oscar seemed quite horrid, always insisting on following the rules, no matter what."

"Some of the rules seemed quite arbitrary as well."

"Such as no drinks after midnight," Bessie suggested. "If someone is thirsty, he or she should be allowed to have a drink, no matter the time."

Andrew nodded. "Oscar didn't have an alibi, but I'm not sure he had a motive."

"If Oscar had been the one killed, there wouldn't be any shortage of suspects with motives."

"Including you, apparently," Andrew teased.

Bessie laughed. "I just hope that when we read the updates, Oscar has moved into a new career field, one that doesn't involve looking after other people."

"That just leaves the neighbour, Herbert Watts," Andrew said.

"I can't understand how he and Larry could have fought for years and years over a fence."

"You've clearly always had good neighbours."

"I have, yes. But surely it would have been easier and less stressful if they had reached some sort of agreement when the matter first arose?"

"It would have, but I got the impression from the interview that Herbert rather enjoyed arguing with Larry."

Bessie sighed. "I have to agree, even though I don't understand it. I hate arguing with anyone."

The pair chatted about the various suspects for a short while longer before Bessie found herself yawning far too frequently. She let Andrew out and then checked that everything was as she wanted it on the ground floor before she climbed the stairs to bed.

CHAPTER 6

*B*essie's internal alarm woke her just a few minutes past six the next morning. She threw back the duvet and got out of bed quickly before she could be tempted to try to get back to sleep. Going back to sleep wasn't something she usually did, but today the idea was oddly appealing. A nice hot shower helped wake her up properly.

After her shower, she sat in her bedroom and patted on the rose-scented dusting powder that reminded her of the man she'd loved and lost many decades earlier.

"How would I have felt if he'd ended up marrying my sister?" she asked her reflection as she combed her hair. It was an impossible question to answer, so the woman in the mirror wisely ignored it.

Bessie was standing in the kitchen, trying to decide whether she should have breakfast before or after her walk, when someone knocked on her door. Assuming it was either Andrew or Helen, or maybe both of them, she opened the door.

"Andy?" she said, trying not to sound as surprised as she was.

THE IRVING FILE

He shrugged and then smiled at her. "I'm back," he said, holding out his arms.

Bessie stepped into the hug, squeezing the young man tightly. "It's so good to see you again," she told him as he released her.

"Is it? I thought maybe you might still be mad at me for being such an idiot."

Bessie shook her head. "You made the mistake of trusting someone who wasn't worthy of your trust. I could never be angry at you for that."

Andy sighed. "You make it sound so much simpler than it actually is. I was an idiot, and I wouldn't blame you one bit if you were angry with me."

Bessie had known Andy Caine since his childhood. Like Hugh, he'd spent a lot of time at Bessie's during his teen years, trying to escape from an unhappy home. The man he'd thought was his father was an alcoholic who wasn't much interested in Andy. Andy's mother loved Andy dearly, but she'd needed to work multiple jobs to keep a roof over their heads while her husband spent nearly all of his time holding down a bar stool at the local pub. Just a few years earlier, Andy had been shocked to learn the truth about his parentage. His father was actually the son of one of the island's wealthiest men. Andy discovered that only when he'd found out that he'd inherited the man's estate.

The inheritance had allowed Andy to finally chase his dreams. He'd gone across to culinary school for a few years and then returned to the island, determined to buy a house and open his own restaurant. In the months following his return, he'd become involved both personally and professionally with Elizabeth Quayle, the youngest child and only daughter of some of Bessie's wealthiest friends.

Elizabeth had dropped out of several different universities before she'd decided to start a party planning business on the island. With Andy acting as her caterer, her business had quickly become a huge success. She and Andy had been looking at houses and planning to move in together when they'd found a dead body in the bedroom of one of the houses they were considering.

The murdered man had been a close friend of Elizabeth's father, George, and once the murderer was behind bars, George and his wife, Mary, had decided to take an extended holiday from the island. Elizabeth had gone with them, ending her relationship with Andy before she went.

It wasn't long before Andy had become involved with someone else. The woman was calling herself Jennifer Johnson, and she did everything she could to come between Andy and Elizabeth, including telling Andy that the real reason that Elizabeth had left the island was because she was pregnant with another man's child.

Andy and Jennifer were actually engaged before Jennifer's lies finally came tumbling down around her and she'd left the island. Not long after her departure, Andy had gone as well, heading to Canada for a change of scenery while he tried to work out what he wanted to do next. Bessie was currently doing everything that she could to help Elizabeth re-establish her business and move on with her life. Of course, she'd do the same for Andy.

"That's enough of that," Bessie said firmly. "I'm just glad you're back. How was Canada? That is where you went, isn't it?"

"I spent some time in Canada and some time in the US," Andy told her. "It was good. I visited some wonderful restaurants, some okay restaurants, and some terrible restaurants. I've come back with lots of ideas for the things that I want to do and quite a bit of knowledge of the things that I don't want to do."

"And now you're back and ready to start looking again for the perfect location for your restaurant?"

Andy grinned at her. "Shall we talk while we walk? I don't want to get in the way of your morning routine."

"And it appears to be a beautiful summer morning," Bessie added as she glanced out the window at the clear skies outside.

"It's a bit cool, but otherwise perfect," Andy told her.

Bessie pulled on her shoes and a light jacket and then followed Andy outside. After locking her door, she set off across the sand at a brisk pace. Andy rushed to keep up with her.

"I need to start walking more," he said with a laugh as they reached the water's edge.

Bessie turned right and began a slower stroll across the damp, packed sand. "You aren't used to walking on sand," she suggested.

"That's very true. I was most recently in New York City for three weeks. I did a lot of walking, but all of it was on pavements and streets."

They walked in silence for a few minutes, until they were past the stairs that led to Thie yn Traie, the large mansion that was perched on the cliff above the beach. George and Mary owned Thie yn Traie, and Bessie knew that the house held many memories for Andy.

"Where were we?" he asked, shaking his head.

"You were telling me about your plans now that you're back on the island."

"I'm going to be visiting the estate agents this morning. I want to see every listing on the island, or very nearly. I need a house, and I need a building that I can turn into a restaurant. Ideally, I'd like to find both of them before the end of the year."

"That seems ambitious. You've already spent a long time looking and couldn't find anything you wanted to buy."

Andy sighed. "I wasn't properly motivated before. When Lizzy and I were together, there just didn't seem to be any rush to buy anything. I stayed with her at Thie yn Traie a lot. She has a huge suite of rooms in a wing that's larger than most of the houses on the island. And catering events for her let me cook and bake without adding any of the pressure of running my own business."

"She may consider working with you again."

"I don't want to work with her again, at least not yet. While I was travelling, I had a lot of time to think. My whole life, I struggled to make ends meet, and I dreamed of owning my own restaurant and my own little cottage on the beach." He glanced at her and flushed. "Treoghe Bwaane felt like home to me more than my mother's cottage. I would love to buy something similar."

Bessie's cottage had already been named Treoghe Bwaane when she'd purchased it. The words were Manx for Widow's Cottage, and the name had felt exactly right to Bessie as she'd mourned the loss of the man she'd loved.

"I don't know of any cottages for sale on the island right now," she told Andy.

He nodded. "Which means I'm going to have to be open to other options. Otherwise, I'll be making my mother crazy, staying with her in her tiny cottage forever."

"She loves having you there."

"She does, but she'll also admit that the cottage is really too small for both of us. Besides, when I'm there, I keep talking about all the changes I want to make, and she loves the cottage exactly as it is. We'll both be happier when I find somewhere else to live."

"So you're looking for a house."

"And a restaurant. I've also realised that I'm being far too particular about that. The only way I'm ever going to know if I can make it as a chef and restaurant owner is if I actually open a restaurant. And you know what? My first restaurant doesn't have to be everything that I've ever dreamed of having. I can start small and then expand or relocate once I've worked out exactly what I want to do. What I can't do is keep sitting around on my ar, er, bottom, waiting for the perfect building and the perfect cottage to become available."

Bessie smiled at him. "It sounds as if your time away was good for you."

"I needed to think, especially after everything that happened with Jennifer. I truly thought that I was in love with her, you know, but while I was gone, I realised that I didn't miss her at all. The only thing being with her had done was let me ignore how much I missed Elizabeth."

He stopped and ran a hand over his eyes. "I still miss Elizabeth," he said softly. "But I don't blame her for not ever wanting to see me again. I never should have believed all of the horrible lies that Jennifer told me about her."

"What's done is done," Bessie told him. "Don't waste your time living with your regrets."

"How is she?"

"Busy. She's been working hard at restarting her business, and that seems to be going well. She's still spending a lot of time with her mother as well."

Mary had fallen ill not long after they'd left the island on their holiday, and the family had spent much of the six months that they'd been away seeking medical treatments for her.

"I'd love to see Mary," Andy said. "She's a wonderful woman. I was so sorry to hear that she'd been ill."

"She's recovering, but slowly. She still doesn't have much strength and she rarely leaves the house."

Andy chuckled. "No doubt that suits her down to the ground. It would drive George crazy."

George was a loud, gregarious man who liked everyone he met and loved socialising. Mary was quiet and shy and enjoyed nothing more than being at home with her children and grandchildren.

"We should probably turn around," Bessie suggested as the row of new houses came into view. Her tummy was starting to rumble, and she was beginning to regret not inviting Andy to join her for breakfast before their walk.

"If you hear of anything that might be coming up for sale, either business or residential, please let me know," Andy told Bessie as they headed back towards her cottage.

"Have you completely given up the idea of buying the Looney mansion, then?"

"I have, although it's been removed from sale, so even if I hadn't, I still wouldn't be able to buy it."

"Removed from sale? I wonder why."

"Maybe all of the families involved are dragging one another to court over ownership."

"Maybe," Bessie said. "It's such a shame that the house will have to sit empty again until things are sorted, though. It was built with such love and meant to be a family home."

"I was serious about a cottage. I'd love nothing more than something right on the beach, and I don't mind if whatever I buy needs a lot of work. I know there won't be anything on Laxey Beach, but the island has many miles of coastline. Someone, somewhere, might be interested in selling a little bit of it."

Bessie thought for a moment. "I can ring a few friends, but I don't know of anyone thinking about selling right now. There are a lot of flats being built in Douglas along the promenade."

"Yeah, Jennifer dragged me around several of the buildings. I'm not especially interested in a modern flat, although I may consider one if I don't find anything else in the next few months. I think Mum and I can live together until Christmas, but anything after that might be too much."

Bessie laughed. "You know you can always stay in my spare room for a night or two."

"Or ten or twenty. Did you ever count how many nights I stayed with you over the years?"

"Of course not. You stayed with me when you needed to get away. It didn't matter how rarely or how often that was – not to me, anyway."

"It bothered my mother, but she wasn't in a position to do anything about it."

"I'm sorry if it bothered Anne. I never meant to upset her."

"She knew that, but I didn't make it easy for her, either. I'm afraid I used to tell her endlessly how much better life was at your cottage. Of course, her husband was the problem, but she didn't want to acknowledge that."

"She did the best she could under the circumstances."

"I know, and I was an ungrateful, um, brat."

Bessie unlocked her cottage door and then she and Andy went inside.

"And now, shall I make you some breakfast?" he asked, opening the refrigerator to see what was inside.

"I was just going to have some toast and fruit," Bessie told him.

He nodded as he moved over to the cupboards and began opening and shutting them.

"And tea," Bessie added, picking up the kettle.

Andy gently took the kettle out of her hand. He filled it with fresh water and switched it on. "Apple-spice pancakes with maple syrup and bacon, or an omelet?" he asked her.

"Oh, goodness, those both sound wonderful. Which would you prefer?"

"Pancakes. I had probably a hundred different plates of pancakes when I was in the US and Canada, and I've been working on several different recipes since I've been back. I think the apple-spice is probably my favourite, but I need other opinions."

"Is your restaurant going to be open for breakfast?"

Andy shrugged. "I know I'm getting way ahead of myself, worrying about different menu items when I don't even have a building yet, but I love fussing over food, and I hate looking at buildings and trying to reimagine the spaces."

"If you want pancakes, make pancakes," Bessie said. "And while you work, we can talk about what you want in a building for your business."

"I wish I knew," Andy told her as he began peeling an apple.

The pair were discussing locations when someone knocked on the door.

"Good morning," Andrew said when Bessie answered his knock. "Helen and I were wondering if you've already had your walk this morning?"

"I have, and now Andy is making me breakfast," Bessie told him.

Andy waved from across the room. "There's going to be plenty of extra, if you'd be interested in trying apple-spice pancakes," he said.

Andrew and Helen exchanged glances.

"Yes, please," Helen said eagerly.

Andrew laughed. "I had a small bowl of some of the cereal that we brought with us for us for my breakfast this morning. I'm still hungry, and even if I weren't, I wouldn't pass up apple-spice pancakes. They sound delicious."

Bessie performed the necessary introductions before Helen and Andrew joined her at the kitchen table.

"Andy is going to be opening his own restaurant on the island soon," she told the others. "He just has to find the right location first."

"I would have thought that Douglas would be the best place for a restaurant," Helen said. "I mean, it's the largest town, isn't it? And that's where most of the businesses are located, so you'd get business lunches and business dinners, and Christmas parties in December."

Andy nodded. "Douglas has a lot to offer, and it's probably my best option, but I can't help but feel as if I'd be happier closer to Laxey."

"You could still live in Laxey, couldn't you?" Helen asked.

"I could, but it makes more sense for me to live close to the restaurant, especially for the first few years. Starting a new restaurant demands a lot of time and effort. The shorter my commute, the more time I have to spend at the restaurant."

"Which could be a bad thing," Andrew suggested. "It might be better if you put some physical distance between yourself and the restaurant. Otherwise, you may find that you spend far too much time there."

Andy sighed and then began mixing together all of the pancake ingredients he'd been carefully measuring. He didn't speak again until he'd poured the first pancake into the waiting pan. As it began to sizzle softly, he looked at Andrew.

"You may be right. I suppose I need to see whether I find a house first or a location for the business first and then go from there. I'm going to start looking today, though, for both of them."

"Would you be happy living in Douglas?" Bessie asked.

"I wish I knew. I didn't want to even consider it when Jennifer and I were looking at houses, but I think that was more to do with not wanting to live with Jennifer than anything else. I just didn't want to admit that to anyone, not even myself. When Elizabeth and I were together, we looked at a few properties in Douglas, but none of them were quite right. At the moment, I think I'm going to have to keep an open mind and see what's available."

"House prices have been going up quite rapidly over the past few years," Bessie said. "The island is suddenly a very popular place to live."

"I'd love to think that people are starting to appreciate all of the things that make it so special, but I suspect it's more to do with the changes that have been made in income tax than anything else," Andy replied.

Andrew laughed. "I've been tempted by them myself," he admitted. "I started looking at houses a few months ago, but life got in the way. I should probably ring the estate agent with whom I was working and have him send me some new listings."

"I'm not certain you should be considering moving to the island," Helen said.

"I'm thinking of buying a second home here," Andrew told her. "I'd keep the flat in London, too, but that's a worry for another day. For now, I'm more interested in breakfast."

Andy grinned as he flipped another pancake. He opened the cooker and looked inside. "The bacon is nearly done, and I've enough pancakes ready for everyone to have two to start. Give me one more minute and I'll start serving."

Bessie got out a jar of maple syrup and made tea. Five minutes later the foursome were digging into fluffy pancakes and crispy bacon.

"Delicious," Bessie said after her first bite. "The spice goes nicely with the sweetness of the syrup."

"I love the apple flavour," Helen said. "I didn't expect to taste so much of the fruit, but I definitely can."

"The pancakes are good, but the bacon is excellent," Andrew said.

Andy laughed. "All I did was stick that in the cooker. It was no work at all."

They all ate until they were stuffed. Helen insisted on helping Andy with the washing-up, leaving Bessie and Andrew to sip their tea and chat.

"What are you planning to do with the rest of your morning?" he asked Bessie.

"I need to go back through the case file," she replied quietly, glancing over at Andy to make sure he wasn't listening. "I want to read everything much more carefully and take notes."

"Do you want to go for lunch somewhere before our meeting?"

Bessie sighed. "I'm incredibly full, but I suppose I'll be hungry again in a few hours. Why don't you just come here and join me for sandwiches?"

"That sounds good. I don't normally eat much breakfast, but I couldn't stop myself today."

When the kitchen was tidy again, Andy gave Bessie a big hug and then rushed away. Helen and Andrew weren't far behind.

"I'll be back around midday," Andrew told Bessie. "Thank you for allowing us to join you for breakfast."

CHAPTER 7

Bessie read the case file, taking notes as she went along, until just before midday. She was in the kitchen, getting out what would be needed for sandwiches, when Andrew and Helen arrived.

"I hope you don't mind that I invited Helen to join us for lunch," he said as Bessie stepped back to let them into the cottage. "I know you've been studying the case file all morning. I thought you could use a break from the case and that if I came alone, you'd want to discuss it."

Bessie grinned at him. "You're right, of course. I do need a break, and if Helen weren't here I probably wouldn't want to take one. I'm very glad you invited her to join us."

The trio made themselves sandwiches and then sat together around the kitchen table. They started talking about books that had been turned into terrible movies, a conversation that made time fly past. Bessie was surprised when she realised that it was almost time for them to leave for Ramsey for their unit meeting.

"Of course, some books have been turned into very good

movies," Helen said. "We can talk about those next time. For now, you and my father need to get to Ramsey."

Bessie nodded. Helen cleared the table and insisted on doing the washing-up while Bessie went upstairs to get ready to go. When Bessie came back down, Helen gave her a quick hug and then they all left together. The drive to Ramsey didn't take long.

"You're in the penthouse today," Jasper Coventry called to them as they walked into the Seaview's large lobby.

Bessie grinned at him. "It's my favourite room in your gorgeous hotel full of wonderful spaces."

"I'm quite fond of it myself," Jasper said as he crossed the room to greet Bessie with a hug. "When Stuart and I first toured the property, before we'd decided to buy it, the estate agent started the tour with the top floor. As soon as I saw the penthouse conference room, I knew I wanted to buy the place and return it to its former glory."

"You've done a wonderful job," Andrew told him.

"We love it, but we also hate it sometimes," Jasper said with a laugh. "But you need to get to your meeting. The new pastry chef couldn't sleep last night, so he came here and started trying out some new ideas. I've given you some samples. Let me know what you think once you've tried them."

"I knew I shouldn't have had that second sandwich," Andrew said with a sigh as he and Bessie boarded the lift.

"I only had one and I'm regretting it. Samples from the pastry chef? How wonderful is that?"

The door to the conference room was open. Hugh was already at the table with a very full plate of food in front of him. He looked up from his plate as Bessie and Andrew walked into the room.

"I came early so that I could get some homework done," he explained. "I was going to work in the library, but Jasper told me to come up here and start working my way through some of the new pudding samples. I, um, couldn't say no to that."

Bessie laughed. "I don't blame you. But what do we have?"

"They're all bite-sized versions of popular puddings," Hugh told her. "So, tiny, bite-sized lemon pies, chocolate cakes, sticky toffee puddings, jam roly-polies, and more."

Bessie looked at the small round balls next to the card that said "Lemon Pie." "Is the outside all pie crust?" she asked.

Hugh nodded. "And the inside is lemon custard or something similar. They're delicious. Actually, everything on the table is delicious, and I've tried at least one of everything."

Bessie filled a plate with several of the selections and then carried the plate to the table. Then she went back and got herself a cup of tea. Andrew took one of everything to go with his tea. They were just walking back to their seats when John and Doona arrived.

"Jasper said something about pudding samples," Doona said excitedly.

"Help yourself," Andrew told her. "There's plenty for everyone."

Charles and Harry arrived a short while later. Charles got himself a cup of coffee. Harry just went and sat with his back to the wall. Ken walked in a few minutes later.

"I'm sorry I'm late," he said as he shut the door behind himself. "It took longer than I thought it would to get here from Lonan."

"We're all enjoying the puddings," Andrew replied. "We didn't even notice you were late."

Ken put a few things on a plate and poured himself some coffee before he joined the others at the table.

"Anyone want to share any initial thoughts?" Andrew asked once Ken was settled.

"I want to know why Amelia and Larry stayed married

for so long," Doona said. "They were both cheating, so clearly neither of them was happy. Why stay together?"

"Does it really matter?" Harry asked. "Amelia didn't kill him."

"If she didn't have an unbreakable alibi, I'd have suspected her," Ken said. "She started out telling the police how much she loved her husband, but then, when she started talking about Eric, she couldn't stop talking about much she loved him and how she wanted them to be together."

"I wish you would have given us the updates on everyone," Doona told Andrew. "I'm dying to know what happened next."

A few people nodded as Andrew chuckled. "You'll be pleased to hear that I haven't read the updates yet either and that I'm going to give them to you before we leave today. Inspector Harrison has given me a brief summary of where everyone is now that I'll share with you later. Before we get to that, though, it may be useful to talk about where we think everyone might be now."

"Amelia isn't a suspect, of course, but I'd like to talk about her," Doona said. "I felt sorry for her when I read the transcript from when she rang 999. Most of that sympathy disappeared when she started talking about Eric, though. She insisted that they were madly in love and that she'd been planning to leave Larry for him."

"Even though she'd not actually done anything that suggests that she was thinking about leaving," Charles said.

Doona nodded. "And Eric was quite adamant that he and Amelia were just having a bit of fun and that he had never even hinted that he was considering leaving his wife for her."

"And did that make you feel sorry for Amelia again?" Ken asked Doona.

She shook her head. "Not really. Once she started talking about how much better in every way Eric was to Larry, I started actively disliking her. Even if she was correct about everything she said, her husband had just been murdered. She could have been a bit nicer when talking about him."

"I'm not certain why she started out saying how much she loved Larry and then spent the second half of the interview complaining about him," Harry said. "If this were my case, I'd be tempted to have another go at breaking her alibi."

Ken nodded. "That was my thought exactly. If she didn't kill him, I wonder if she paid someone else to do it."

"Where is she now?" Bessie asked.

"Let's talk about a few of the suspects before we start down that road," Andrew suggested. "Anything I tell you about Amelia will also tell you things about some of the others – people we have yet to discuss."

"We were just talking about Eric," Harry said. "I didn't care for him, but I can't really find a solid motive for him. He was having an affair with Amelia, but I didn't get the impression that he cared about her."

Charles nodded. "He came across as rather unpleasant. I think he loved his wife, at least to some extent, but I didn't get the impression that he cared about Amelia much at all. She was attractive and willing, so he slept with her when the opportunity arose, but their relationship wasn't anything more to him, or so it seemed."

Bessie frowned. "You make it all sound rather awful."

"When I read Eric's statement, it didn't seem quite that bad to me," Doona said. "But I can see why you felt that way, and you may be correct. I certainly didn't care for Eric after I read what he said in his interview. Now that we're talking about him, I'm starting to actively dislike him."

"Does anyone here think that Eric was actually considering leaving his wife for Amelia?" Andrew asked.

A few people shook their heads.

"Not at all," Harry said.

"Not really," Bessie replied. "Having said that, I'm not certain that I believe that Amelia was planning to leave Larry, either. I think Amelia's emotions got the better of her during the interview. Perhaps, as the interview went on, the reality of the situation gradually started to sink in and she just started babbling."

"That's possible," Andrew said. "Eric was a good deal calmer."

"Which made me wonder why he'd been so easily upset at the conference," Doona said. "There were hundreds of witnesses who said that he was speechless and overwhelmed when Janice confronted him. I couldn't help but contrast that to his police interview. He came across as someone completely in control of his emotions while being questioned."

"Perhaps the police would have seen a different side of him if they'd let his wife interview him about the murder," Hugh suggested.

Everyone chuckled.

"So no one cared for Eric?" Andrew asked.

"I didn't care for him, but I don't think he killed Larry," John said. "For one thing, getting back to Wellington and then returning to Auckland would have taken a lot of time and effort. Eric didn't seem the type to expend that much effort, not unless he was certain of financial gain from it."

Andrew nodded. "He did spend quite a lot of his interview talking about how successful he was."

"He has his own plane, or he did have then," Doona said.

"He was a very successful senior manager for a large pharmaceutical company. He was very well compensated for his work," Ken said. "I don't think I read anything in the files about the plane, but I'd like to know if it was actually his plane or if it belonged to the company and he simply had use of it. If it was the company's plane, I doubt he would have used it to fly back to Wellington to murder his lover's husband."

Andrew made a note. "He does talk about the plane as if it was his, but it's worth verifying the actual ownership. Is Eric on anyone's short list of suspects?"

"He's on my short list, but he isn't at the top," Harry replied. "But then my short list includes everyone who was on Inspector Harrison's list."

"From the information that we have so far, I can't see him being the killer," Hugh said. "I don't think he cared enough about Amelia to murder anyone on her behalf."

"Could he have wanted Larry dead for some other reason?" Bessie asked. "Is it possible that Larry knew about the affair and had threatened to tell Janice? There could be dozens of other possibilities, I suppose."

Andrew nodded. "Before we start making a list of all of them, let's move on. We can revisit Eric once we know more about where he is now."

"Janice," Doona said. "I wanted to feel sorry for her. I did feel sorry for her for about five minutes, actually, but then I kept reading and I started to think that she was as horrible as all the others."

"It seemed obvious to me that she'd only married Eric for his money," Harry said.

Bessie winced. "I wouldn't say that."

"She was definitely more worried about what she might get from her divorce settlement than about Larry's murder," Harry said. "The police had great difficulty getting her to answer their questions."

"To be fair, she'd only just found out that her husband was cheating on her," Doona said. "She may well have been overwhelmed by everything that had happened over the past twenty-four hours or so."

"Can we see Janice as a suspect?" Andrew asked.

"Only if she killed Larry to get back at Amelia," Doona said. "Which is a possibility, but a very sad one."

"She and Amelia were friends before Janice found out about the affair. What if Amelia had been telling Janice all sorts of horrible stories about Larry? Maybe she told Janice that Larry hit her or was actually a pedophile or some such thing," Charles said. "Perhaps Janice killed him to try to save her friend."

"I think that's a stretch," Ken said.

"Bessie also suggested that she might have killed Larry to get back at Amelia for sleeping with Eric," Andrew said. "She also wondered whether Janice was lying about when she found out about the affair. Maybe she knew days or even weeks before she confronted Eric."

"I think we all agree that she had a motive," Ken said. "Even if it wasn't the strongest of motives. That doesn't change regardless of when she found out about the affair."

"She's on my list, and she's higher on it than her husband, actually," Harry said. "That's all subject to change once we find out where everyone is now."

Andrew glanced at the clock. "Let's keep going, then. What did you think of Rosie?"

"She seemed to find the entire thing amusing," Harry said. "I don't think she cared enough about Larry to kill him, and I hope she's somewhere doing something wonderful now."

Doona nodded. "She was the most likeable of the bunch, which isn't saying much. She said she and Larry were just having a bit of fun together, and I can't see any reason to doubt her."

"She's at the bottom of my list, unless we learn something about where she is now to change that," Charles said.

"I'm inclined to agree," Andrew said. "What did you all think of James?"

"I want to know why he and Larry were talking again

after twelve years apart," Doona said. "Larry and Amelia were still together. What changed to make him no longer angry with Larry? Did he know that Amelia was having an affair? Did he know that Larry was having an affair? Did Larry tell him about Rosie? Would James have been upset to hear that Larry was cheating on Amelia, considering that James claimed to still be in love with her? I could go on."

Andrew smiled at her. "I'd rather you didn't at this point. I think it's clear that James wasn't questioned thoroughly enough. That's one of the first things I want Inspector Harrison to correct."

"He's low on my list," Harry said. "But if we find out that he and Amelia are together now, he'll move up."

Charles nodded. "I feel the same way. I don't think he killed his brother, but he did admit in his interview after Larry's death that he felt as if he was just as much in love with Amelia then as he had been twelve or thirteen years earlier."

"I don't want them to be together," Doona said. "I think James can do a lot better. I liked him a lot more than I liked Amelia."

Bessie nodded. "I felt the same."

"Let's talk about Oscar," Harry suggested. "Did anyone like him?"

A few people laughed.

"I hope he's not still working for the same place," Bessie said. "I really hope he's doing something that doesn't involve interacting with people in any way, but that may be too much to ask."

"I didn't care for him, but I can't imagine why he would have killed Larry," Charles said. "It seemed likely that he was going to get Larry fired before much longer. Once he'd managed that, he wouldn't have had to see Larry ever again."

"Unless they had some shared history about which we

know nothing," Hugh said. "Maybe they'd been at school together, or maybe they were sixth cousins or something."

"The police did investigate Larry's past as much as they could," Andrew said. "They didn't find anything to suggest that Larry and Oscar had ever met prior to Oscar's taking the job in Wellington."

"Someone should ask Oscar why he disliked Larry so much," Bessie said. "I mean, it seems as if Oscar was simply obsessed with following the rules and with making everyone else follow them too, but maybe there was more to it than that."

Doona nodded. "When Oscar was questioned, he said that he got along with Larry about the same as he got along with everyone else at the care home. Was that actually the case, though? Was Oscar giving everyone written warnings all the time, or did he single out Larry for some reason? I suppose it's possible that every other employee was following all of the rules exactly, but I don't think it's likely."

"Rosie might be a good source for finding out more about Oscar and his relationship with Larry," Ken said. "Unless Rosie and Oscar are together now, in which case, she'll move up the list of suspects in my mind."

"You think Rosie killed Larry to make Oscar happy?" Harry asked.

Ken shrugged. "No, not really, but if the pair are together now, or got together for a while after Larry's death, then it might be a possibility."

"That just leaves Herbert Watts," Andrew said. "Thoughts?"

"He seemed quite sad when he was told that Larry had died," Doona said. "He said something about not having anyone to argue with any longer."

"Which is odd," Hugh said.

"He did admit that he and Larry had been arguing for

years over the fence between their properties. Herbert didn't seem to see that as a possible motive for Larry's murder," Ken said.

"He also said that he barely knew Amelia, which seems odd considering how long she and Larry had lived in the house," Bessie added.

"I found it interesting that he knew all about Rosie," Hugh said. "She thought they'd been very discreet, but Herbert had seen her going in and out of the house at all hours of the day and night for nearly two years. Maybe if Amelia had bothered to get to know Herbert better, he would have told her that Larry was cheating."

"He didn't know anything about Amelia and Eric, though," John said. "Amelia said they never met at her house or at Eric's."

"Whereas Rosie used to come over to see Larry whenever Amelia was travelling for work," Doona said. "And Amelia travelled quite a bit."

"And Eric often travelled with her," Hugh added. "Which gave them plenty of opportunity to be together."

"Where is Herbert on everyone's list?" Andrew asked.

"My problem is that everyone is near the bottom of the list," Harry told him. "I don't actually have anyone at the top of the list, although I'd put Amelia there if I could."

Bessie nodded. "I agree. She seems to have had the strongest motive. Maybe she did pay someone to kill her husband."

"If she didn't, then maybe the police missed something huge, like another suspect with a strong motive," Harry said. "They may need to go back and dig deeper into Larry's job, his past, and his family."

Andrew made a note. "Before we go any further down that path, let's take a quick look at where everyone is now."

CHAPTER 8

"Does anyone want to guess whether Amelia and Eric ended up together?" Andrew asked.

"No chance," Doona said. "He'll have done everything in his power to keep his marriage together, but even if he and Janice didn't stay together, there's no way he and Amelia are together now."

"Does anyone disagree?" Andrew asked.

A few people shook their heads.

"From what I read, I'd be shocked if he was with Amelia now," Bessie said.

"He is not," Andrew admitted. "Let's start with Amelia. She sold the house almost immediately and bought a small flat on the opposite side of the city. I'll be giving you copies of her entire interview, but Inspector Harrison summarised it by saying that she's spent the last five years moving in and out of very short-lived relationships." He stopped and then looked up at them. "And that's all I know about Amelia at this point. As I said earlier, this is just a summary. I haven't read the full reports yet."

"None of what you've said surprises me," Harry said.

"Me either," Ken said. "I wouldn't have been surprised if you'd said she'd sworn off men after Larry's death, either, but what you said was just as likely."

"What about Eric, then?" Doona asked.

"Eric is still working the same job. He and Janice got divorced, and she got primary custody of the children. Eric has remained single since the divorce was finalised, and he told Inspector Harrison that he wasn't interested in ever getting married again," Andrew replied.

"He's still in the same job," Doona repeated. "What about Amelia?"

Andrew checked his notes. "She's also still working in the same job for the same company."

"So she's still working for Eric, even after everything that happened," Doona said. "I wasn't expecting that."

"If I were her, I'd have found another job," Hugh said.

"Maybe Eric should have been the one who found another job," Doona replied. "He was her supervisor. They shouldn't have been involved in the first place."

"What about Janice?" Bessie asked. "You said she got custody of the children?"

"She did, and as soon as the ink was dry on the divorce decree, she moved with them to Auckland. Three months later, she got married again," Andrew told them.

"Three months?" Doona echoed. "She must have been seeing her new husband behind Eric's back when they were married, then."

"According to Inspector Harrison, they met only after the divorce," Andrew replied. "Apparently, Janice admitted that they'd had something of a whirlwind romance, but she insisted that she didn't regret their decision to get married after only three months. She claims they're still very happy together, over four years later."

"Is there any connection between her new husband and Larry?" Harry asked.

"Not that Inspector Harrison mentioned," Andrew replied.

"Fascinating," Harry said. "I can't wait to read her complete interview."

"Rosie next, please," Doona said. "I really want to hear how happy she is not being involved with Larry any longer."

"Rosie has moved jobs a few times since Larry's death," Andrew said. "She's currently working as a private nurse for a wealthy family where the grandmother is unwell. According to Inspector Harrison, she's involved with two different men and isn't serious about either of them."

"Good for her," Doona said.

"What about James? I do hope he's finally over Amelia," Bessie said after she'd added the notes about Rosie to her notebook.

"From what Inspector Harrison could determine, James is actually still in love with Amelia," Andrew replied, sighing. "He's still working the same job and living in the same place."

"The poor man needs to move on," Bessie said.

Hugh nodded. "Even I can see that, and I'm clueless when it comes to women."

Everyone laughed.

"What about Oscar?" Ken asked. "I hope he's now working somewhere away from people."

"Apparently, he's changed jobs about a half-dozen times in the past five years," Andrew said. "He's stayed in care home administration, though. Inspector Harrison reckons that the first few jobs were more or less lateral moves, but he suspects that Oscar has been slowly sliding down to positions with fewer responsibilities and, one would assume, lower pay ever since."

"Let's hope he's learning to treat his staff better, then," Bessie said.

Andrew nodded. "We may find out more from his full interview."

"Which just leaves Herbert for last again," Bessie said. "We really must make an effort to talk about him first at least once."

"If I were a suspect in a murder investigation, I'd be quite happy to be the last suspect everyone talked about," Ken said.

Bessie chuckled. "You have a point."

"Herbert is still living in the same house," Andrew said. "He told Inspector Harrison that he still misses Larry. The inspector noted that Herbert tried asking Amelia out after the funeral, but Amelia turned him down."

"That's kind of creepy," Doona said. "I hope he didn't mean immediately after the funeral, like the same day."

"I'm not sure, but it's probably in the full interviews, either Amelia's or Herbert's or both," Andrew replied.

"Is that everyone the inspector interviewed again?" Harry asked.

"It is. He's eager to get our list of questions and then go back and speak to everyone again. He's also happy to talk to anyone else that we can identify as a person of interest," Andrew said. "Does anyone have any questions for him at this point?"

"I still want to know why Amelia stayed with Larry," Doona said. "Even if she were planning to leave him, why had she stayed with him up to that point? It seems as if they were miserable together."

Andrew made a note. "Anyone else?"

"Do you think he'd be willing to have another go at breaking Amelia's alibi?" Harry asked.

Andrew shook his head. "He was adamant in his initial email that there was no way that Amelia killed Larry. He did admit that she could have hired someone to do the job, but he couldn't find any evidence to suggest that Amelia would have been able to find a contract killer or that she could have afforded to pay one the going rate."

"I assume someone has compared the crime to similar crimes in their database," Harry said.

"I can ask him. I don't know that their database is computerised, but I also don't think they have many murders to deal with each year," Andrew replied.

"I have questions about all of them, but I'd like to read the updated interviews first," Hugh said. "We're meeting again the day after tomorrow, aren't we?"

Andrew nodded. "I'll send an email to Inspector Harrison tonight, letting him know that we're working on the case. I'll add Doona's question, but I'll probably suggest that he wait to talk to Amelia again until after we've next met. I suspect we'll have a great many more questions for him at that point."

"Is that all for today, then?" Harry asked, shutting his notebook.

Andrew flipped through the pile of envelopes in front of him and pulled one out. "Here's your copy of the recent interviews," he said, handing the envelope to Harry. "We'll meet again the day after tomorrow at the same time."

"Jasper left boxes," Hugh said. "And he told me to tell everyone to take puddings with them."

"I'm good, but thanks," Harry said as he headed for the door.

"I'll have a few things," Charles said as he took his envelope from Andrew. He walked to the table and tossed a few treats into a box. He left while the others were still gathering up their things.

"I want all of it," Doona said as she approached the table. "Especially the little round cakes. They were delicious."

"I love that everything is small and round," Bessie said. "I don't think I've ever had round cake before."

"It's the chocolate coating that makes it so good," Hugh said as he joined them. "I'm going to take a bunch home for Grace. Aalish can have one or two as well, but not too many."

"I'd better take some home for my two," John said. "Thomas and Amy are old enough to notice if I'm eating something special."

Hugh laughed. "Aalish will notice if she's awake, but she goes to bed pretty early. I don't know how much longer that will last, but I'm enjoying it while I can."

Bessie filled a box with several of the small balls of cake and pastry. "There wasn't anything I didn't like," she told Doona.

"But the chocolate cake balls were the best," Doona replied.

"They were very good," Bessie said, adding another one to her box.

Andrew filled two boxes. "One is for Helen," he said loudly. "Just in case anyone thinks I'm being greedy."

"We don't care if you are," Ken told him.

"How is the hotel?" Bessie asked Ken.

He shrugged. "It's fine."

"I feel as if there is a 'but' there," Bessie said.

Ken laughed. "It really is fine. It just feels quite isolated, especially as I'm used to living in London. It's very quiet down there, or it was until a few of Harlan's friends turned up at two in the morning."

"Oh dear," Bessie said.

"What did they want at that hour?" Doona asked.

Ken shrugged. "They made a lot of noise, but I couldn't actually hear enough to understand what they were shouting about."

"But it was enough to wake you," Bessie said.

"Actually, I woke up when the cars arrived. One of them was very noisy, either by design or disrepair. I'm not certain which. When both cars stopped, seemingly right outside my door, I got up to see what was happening."

"And what did you see?" Andrew asked.

"Two cars parked near the first room," Ken told him. "Men in dark clothes got out of both cars. They were already shouting about something before they even knocked on Harlan's door."

"Were they shouting at each other or at Harlan?" John asked.

"I wish I knew. Harlan opened his door and shouted something back at them. I thought I heard the word 'guest' in there somewhere, but I'm not certain. They all got a bit quieter after that, anyway."

"What did you do?" Bessie wondered.

"I got back into bed and tried to go back to sleep. They'd all gone into Harlan's room, slamming the door behind them. About ten minutes later, I heard his door open again. It was shut fairly quietly, but then both cars started up and drove away. I struggled to get back to sleep after that."

"How awful. I hope that doesn't happen every night while you're here," Doona said.

"I've asked a colleague in London to see if he can find out anything about Harlan," Andrew said. "I'll let you know as soon as I hear back from him."

"There's no law against having visitors late at night," John said. "But if you're running a hotel, you should be more aware of the needs of your guests."

"If he keeps having noisy, late-night visitors, maybe you should consider coming to stay on Laxey Beach," Bessie said. "I'm sure Harry or Charles could make room for you. I can almost guarantee that it will be quiet at night."

"Did you complain to anyone about the incident?" John

asked.

Ken shook his head. "I would never complain over that sort of thing. As you said, there isn't any law against people having visitors."

"I could have a word with Hilary," Bessie offered. "She'd probably appreciate knowing what's happening at the hotel when she isn't there."

"I don't want to cause any trouble for anyone," Ken said.

"Where does Hilary live?" Andrew asked.

"The family built a large home at the same time as they were building all of their other businesses. It isn't all that far from the hotel, actually. If I'm remembering correctly, when they built it, it had fourteen bedrooms. I remember someone telling me that Donald wanted several children, and they also added rooms for nannies and other staff."

"But they only had two children in the end," Andrew remembered.

"Yes, but the extra rooms came in handy for when the grandchildren used to come to visit years later. I'm certain I would have heard if Hilary had sold the house."

"If she has such a huge house, why isn't Harlan staying there?" Ken asked.

"As they are both unmarried, it wouldn't be appropriate for them to live together, even if they are aunt and nephew," Bessie replied. "It would be different if Harlan had grown up as part of the family, but, as it is, he's a stranger to Hilary. She's right to be cautious and have him stay at the hotel."

"Oh, I think she's absolutely right to have him stay at the hotel," Ken said quickly. "But she seems quite convinced that he's her nephew, so I wondered why he wasn't staying with her."

"I don't think I can fit any more puddings in my box," Doona said sadly, closing the lid. "I think I'll skip dinner and just eat my way through everything in here."

"That's a terrible but very tempting idea," John said. "I was wondering if we should have dinner together to talk about the case, though."

"Just us?" Doona asked with a wink.

John laughed. "We could have dinner, just us, if you'd rather, but I was going to invite Bessie and Hugh and Andrew. And Ken, if you're interested."

Ken smiled. "Thank you, but no. I want to read through the recent interviews and take a few notes, but then I have to start sorting through the various applications from people who are interested in joining my cold case unit. I need to start trying to narrow down the list of possibilities."

He picked up his papers and his box of treats and headed for the door. "I'll see you all the day after tomorrow," he said as he exited the room.

"I'm free for dinner," Bessie said.

"Sadly, I am not," Andrew said. "I'm taking Helen into Douglas to meet up with a friend of hers who recently moved to the island. Feel free to solve the case without me."

Everyone chuckled.

"Why don't you all come to my cottage?" Bessie suggested. "I'll fill an extra box of puddings just for tonight and I'll make spaghetti."

"That sounds wonderful," John said.

"Especially since the restaurant across from the station has gone out of business again and it's currently sitting empty," Doona added.

"It's never been empty for long," Bessie said.

"I know, and now it's been empty for almost a week. I'm starting to get worried," John said.

"Is someone going to invite Hugh?" Bessie asked.

"I'll text him on the drive back to Laxey," Doona told her. "We'll be at your cottage around six."

"I'll start the water boiling, but I won't add the pasta until

I see whether or not Hugh is joining us," Bessie said.

"Because if he is, you'll need twice as much," Doona laughed.

Bessie filled another box with more puddings specifically for the evening ahead. Then she picked up all of her things and looked at Andrew.

"Ready?" she asked.

He picked up his bag and began to put his folders and envelopes away. "Darn it," he exclaimed. "I still have Ken's copies of the recent interviews. How did that happen?"

"I think we all might have been a little too excited about the puddings," Bessie said.

Andrew nodded. "Do you mind stopping at Ken's hotel on our way back to Laxey? I know it isn't on the way, but you know what I mean."

"I do know what you mean, and I don't mind," Bessie assured him. "If we happen to see Hilary, I might have a quick word with her about Harlan as well."

They chatted about the case and their puddings, but mostly their puddings, on the drive.

"I don't see Ken's car," Bessie said as they pulled up in front of the hotel.

"He didn't say he was stopping anywhere on his way back here, but obviously he doesn't have to tell me his plans."

"What should we do?"

Andrew frowned. "I don't want to leave the envelope with Hilary or Harlan. The information in it is classified. I'll ring Ken and see if he answers."

He pulled out his mobile and scrolled through his list of contacts. As he pushed a button and put the phone to his ear, the door to the office swung open. Harlan walked out and walked towards the car, an angry scowl on his face. Bessie tapped Andrew's arm and pointed to the man. Andrew pushed a button to end the call.

"Good afternoon," Andrew said after he'd put his window down. "We were hoping to find my friend, Ken, in his room."

"He's not," Harlan snapped.

"Yes, I realised that when I didn't see his car," Andrew replied. "I was just ringing him to see where he is."

"He's out," Harlan told him.

"We may sit here for a few minutes just in case he turns up. I have something I need to give him," Andrew explained.

"I'll take it," Harlan said quickly.

"That's very kind of you, but I'm afraid that won't work. We'll wait for Ken for a few minutes. I'll keep trying his mobile, too."

Harlan frowned. "Not long."

"Why not?" Bessie demanded. "We aren't causing any trouble sitting here."

Harlan looked past Andrew to give Bessie a hard stare. "Not long," he repeated before turning and walking back towards the office.

"That felt threatening," Bessie said as Harlan slammed the office door.

"It did, didn't it?" Andrew replied. "I'm not certain I want Ken staying here."

"I'm going to ring Hilary. She needs to know that Harlan is threatening people."

Bessie dug out her mobile phone and began looking through her list of contacts. While she was doing that, Andrew tried Ken's number again.

"I don't have the number in my phone," Bessie said eventually. "It will be in my address book at home, though. I'll ring her when I get home."

"Ken isn't answering, and I don't want to sit here all afternoon," Andrew said a moment later. "I'll keep trying to ring him once we get back to Laxey."

As Andrew began to reverse out of his parking space,

another car appeared on the road behind them.

"There's Ken," Bessie said as Andrew stopped his car.

Ken parked next to them and quickly climbed out of his car. "I forgot to grab my updates," he said as he approached Andrew's door.

"I didn't realise until after you'd left," Andrew replied as he handed Ken the envelope.

"I was nearly back here when I remembered, so I turned around and drove back to Ramsey," Ken explained. "Except you were all gone when I got to the Seaview."

"We must have driven past one another at some point, then," Andrew said.

Ken laughed. "I doubt it. I took a completely unplanned but incredibly scenic detour through the countryside. Thank you for bringing this to me. I'm eager to get started."

As Ken walked away, Andrew began reversing again. He'd gone only a few feet when another car appeared. It pulled into the car park and the driver began honking the horn. A moment later, Harlan walked out of the office. He walked around to the passenger door and climbed into the car. The car sped away as Andrew and Bessie watched.

"Hilary must be in the office, then," Bessie said as they watched the car disappear into the distance.

"Do you want to go in and have a word with her?"

"I do, actually." Bessie got out of the car and walked to the office. The door was locked. Frowning, she returned to Andrew's car.

"The sign on the door says that the manager had to step away from the office to help another guest but will be right back," Bessie told Andrew. "I wonder if Hilary knows that Harlan is leaving the hotel unattended?"

"I suspect she'll know soon," Andrew said as he finally managed to reverse fully out of his parking space. They were on their way back to Laxey a moment later.

CHAPTER 9

Back at Treoghe Bwaane, Bessie pulled out her address book and then checked the number she had for Hilary with the latest telephone directory. Then she tried the number. It rang a dozen times before she gave up.

"No one is home," she told Andrew.

"Maybe she was driving the car that came and collected Harlan."

"She never would have just sat there and honked in that way. Besides, I caught a glimpse of the driver. He was a dark-haired man around forty."

"So maybe she was a passenger in that car," Andrew suggested.

"I suppose it's possible that she was sitting in the back and I didn't see her, but if she had been, she would have complained loudly about the honking."

Andrew shrugged. "Do you want to try going to her house?"

"I'll keep trying her number for the rest of today. If she doesn't answer, I'll have to think about what I want to do next. For now, though, I'm eager to start reading the case file."

"I won't stay and bother you, then," Andrew replied. "Enjoy your dinner with your friends. If your lights are on when I get back from Douglas, I may come over to hear how it went."

"We aren't going to solve the case."

"You never know."

Bessie chuckled. "We may come up with a theory about what happened, but we're going to need answers from Inspector Harrison before we'll be able to actually solve the case."

"Make a list of questions. If I can get them from you tonight, I'll email them to him before I go to bed."

"I'll do my best."

Andrew gave her a hug before he left. Bessie watched him walk back to his cottage before she shut her door. Then she brewed herself a cup of tea and sat down with the envelope full of the recent statements. Time seemed to rush past, but she was careful to keep an eye on the clock because she'd promised to make dinner for her friends.

She had the sauce simmering gently and the water just about to boil when Hugh arrived. John and Doona weren't far behind. Bessie added the pasta to the water and then served the salad while they waited for the pasta to cook. A short while later, they all sat down together to enjoy steaming plates full of delicious food.

"This is wonderful," Hugh said after his first bite. "We nearly always get takeaway when we meet. I'd forgotten how well you cook."

Bessie laughed. "I've nearly forgotten how to cook. As you say, we nearly always get takeaway during cases, and I've fallen into the bad habit of buying ready meals and cans of soup when we're between cases, rather than cooking for myself."

"Tell me about it," Doona said. "Between John's schedule and the children's activities, I never cook anymore. Thomas and Amy have said that they want to do some cooking for all of us once school finishes for the summer holidays, but I don't think it will actually happen."

John nodded. "They both really want to help, but they're also busy with friends and other activities. We may get one or two meals out of them before they give up, but it won't be much more than that."

"I'll be thrilled to get two meals," Doona told him.

"I can't imagine Aalish cooking anything," Hugh said. "Grace wants to get her a toy kitchen for Christmas. She's hoping that if Aalish has her own little kitchen, she won't be so eager to be underfoot in our kitchen when Grace is trying to prepare meals."

John laughed. "I remember those days. Toddlers just want to be with their parents all the time. I don't imagine a toy kitchen will do much to distract Aalish, but she will probably have great fun with it when Grace wants to play kitchen with her."

Hugh nodded. "Grace already warned me that I'll probably come home to tea parties every night. I love watching Aalish's imagination grow, though."

They chatted more about Aalish and Amy and Thomas while they ate. John did the washing-up while Doona cleared the table and made tea before she put all of the puddings that Bessie had selected for the evening onto a plate. When she put the plate in the centre of the table, Bessie sighed.

"I loved all of them," she said. "But I know I shouldn't eat another one of each."

"I'm going to have one of each," Hugh said.

"I'm going to stick to the cakes," Doona told them.

Bessie selected a few small treats and then sat back and sipped her tea. "I didn't get as much time as I might have liked with the new interviews," she said as she put her cup down. "But I read through them all at least once."

"I did the same," Doona said. "And then I read a few of them a second time because I was so unsettled by what I'd read the first time."

John nodded. "Some of them were somewhat unsettling, weren't they? I was surprised to feel that way. Andrew had already told us what to expect, but quite a few things in the interviews surprised me."

"Let's talk about each suspect in turn," Hugh suggested. "And I want to start with Oscar, who seems to blame Larry for every bad thing in his life."

Doona nodded. "I was shocked when he said that his life had been almost perfect before Larry got himself killed and that things had been going steadily downhill for him ever since."

"If he did kill Larry, that obviously isn't what he thought would happen as a result," Hugh said.

"We never did come up with much of a motive for the man, did we?" Bessie asked.

"Not unless the men had some shared history about which we know nothing," John said. "It seems as if Oscar was getting close to getting rid of Larry. As far as we can tell, Oscar didn't have any reason to kill him."

"After his most recent interview, I kind of hope he did, though," Hugh said. "I already didn't care for him, and he was even worse in the second interview."

"He was quite awful," Doona agreed. "He complained about his job, his flat, his bad back, and the poor woman he's been seeing for the past three months."

"I found it interesting that he even blamed Larry for his unhappy personal relationship," John said. "He said something about having been able to attract much more intelligent and beautiful women before Larry's death."

"I really didn't understand how any of it was Larry's fault, though," Doona said. "He said something about how Larry should have worked harder and not been murdered, as if the two were connected."

"Which suggests that Larry was killed because of something that happened at work," Hugh said.

"Except I don't think Oscar has any idea why Larry was killed," John said. "He's just blaming Larry for everything that's wrong in his own life."

"Of course none of it is Larry's fault," Bessie said. "Oscar is just the type of person who wants to blame others for his own mistakes and misfortunes. Having said that, I still don't think he had any motive for killing Larry."

"Sadly, he's at the bottom of my list," Doona replied. "I think he's my least favourite suspect, though, so if we can come up with a motive for him, I'd be happy to move him up the list."

Everyone chuckled.

"He's at the bottom of my list, too," Hugh said. "I don't think he killed Larry, but I do think there is something shady about him. I think Inspector Harrison should dig into his background, or maybe even his current situation, a bit more."

John nodded. "I'm inclined to agree. I can't say exactly why, but I didn't care for the man, and, if it were my case, I'd be looking at him very closely, not for Larry's murder, but more generally."

"But we're supposed to be solving Larry's murder," Doona said. "So let's talk about the people who could have done it. People like Eric Price."

"Who came across as miserable and sad," Bessie said. "Although, for all of his insisting that he still loved Janice and wanted her back more than anything, he's still working with Amelia."

"But they aren't still involved," Doona said.

"If I were Janice, I wouldn't even consider taking him back while he was still working with Amelia," Bessie said. "Eric should have quit his job as soon as he got back to Wellington."

"I really think Janice would have left him anyway," John said.

"Probably, but at least he'd be less bitter and angry about having to see Amelia every day," Doona said.

"And he still isn't looking for another job," Hugh added. "He said he plans to stay where he is until he's ready to retire, even if Amelia stays, too."

"I'm not sure why he would have killed Larry, unless Larry had found out about the affair and was threatening to tell Janice," Doona said. "I can absolutely see him killing Larry to try to protect his relationship with Janice."

"We really need to know who rang Janice and told her about the affair," Bessie said.

"She claims, in both interviews, that she didn't recognise the voice and that the caller didn't identify himself or herself," Doona said.

"And I didn't believe her either time," Bessie said. "You don't just drop everything and fly to another city based on an anonymous phone call."

"Who might have rung her?" Hugh asked. "But not just that – who might have rung her whom she would want to protect?"

"That's a good point, actually," John said. "I did wonder if Amelia had rung Janice herself, but I can't see why Janice would lie about who rang if it had been Amelia. I think she'd have been happy to accuse Amelia of ringing, actually."

Hugh nodded. "Who else might it have been, though? Did Janice even know any of the other suspects?"

"I can't see how she could have known Rosie or James," Bessie said thoughtfully. "She claimed she barely knew Larry, after all. Having said that, I can't imagine her knowing Oscar or Herbert, either. Unless she'd known one of them years earlier, which is always possible, I suppose."

"So maybe she truly didn't recognise the voice of the person who rang her," Bessie said. "But maybe she rang someone else after she spoke to the anonymous caller. Maybe she rang someone at the conference and asked them about Eric and Amelia."

"I thought everyone at the conference was shocked when the truth came out," Hugh said.

Bessie sighed. "I still can't imagine her leaving the children with her mother and flying to Auckland as soon as she heard the news. If I were her, I would have packed up all of Eric's things and then had the locks changed."

"Again, you're assuming that she believed the person who rang. Why did she believe him or her?" Doona asked.

"Either he or she was very convincing, or the caller was able to offer some sort of proof," John said.

"What sort of proof?" Bessie asked.

"I wish I knew. Janice was vague when she was asked to try to repeat the entire conversation. There may well have been more to it than what she told the police, though," John replied.

"Regardless of who rang her, I don't think Janice killed Larry," Doona said. "I just can't imagine what she could have been hoping to accomplish by killing the man."

"Maybe she just wanted Amelia to suffer," Hugh suggested.

"But surely she didn't want to do anything that might drive Eric and Amelia closer together," Doona argued.

"What if she killed Larry before she learned that Eric and Amelia were having an affair?" Hugh suggested.

"For what reason?" Doona asked.

Hugh shrugged. "She and Amelia were friends before she found out about the affair, right? Maybe she found out that Larry was cheating, and she wanted to help her friend."

"I can't imagine murdering someone to help out a friend," Doona said. "For now, Janice is near the bottom of my list."

"Mine, too," Bessie said. "Although, out of everyone, she seems to be the happiest with how her life is now."

"But she didn't directly benefit from Larry's death," Doona said. "She's happier because she divorced Eric, which would have happened anyway after she found about the affair."

Bessie nodded. "I did wonder, based on a few things that she said, whether she was thinking about divorcing Eric anyway."

"I don't remember reading anything about that," John said.

Bessie flipped through her notes. "She told the police inspector that she'd had two more children with her second husband, the man who swept her off her feet just a few months after her divorce. She said that she planned to keep having more babies, and then muttered something about Eric not wanting more than the two they had. At least, that's what's in my notes."

Doona looked up from her copy of the interviews. "I didn't really catch that when I read the interview, but you're right. The police inspector noted that she said the part about Eric almost under her breath. I wish he'd pushed her a bit harder on that. If she was planning to divorce Eric anyway, then finding out about the affair was lucky for her. It gave her a good reason to leave, and it sounds as if she was awarded primary custody of their children because of his affair."

"Was I the only one who was shocked at how quickly she'd remarried?" Bessie asked. "I think Inspector Harrison should take a look at her second husband. Is it possible that they were having an affair before she and Eric separated?"

"Even if they were, I can't see why that would give her a reason to kill Larry," Hugh said.

"Maybe Larry found out about that affair and threatened to tell Eric," Doona suggested.

Bessie chuckled. "That may be overcomplicating things."

"We've talked about both Eric and Janice Price. Are either of them high on your list of suspects?" John asked.

Bessie sighed and shook her head. "I simply can't imagine a strong enough motive for either of them," she said.

Hugh nodded. "I can see Eric killing to protect his secret, but we've no reason to believe that Larry knew about the affair or that he'd threatened to tell Janice about it."

"Eric is higher than Janice on my list because Larry might have known about the affair," Doona said. "Who haven't we talked about yet?"

"James," Bessie said. "Who is, sadly, still in love with Amelia. I found his statement difficult to read. He sounded sad and confused and deeply depressed."

"I was shocked to read that Amelia had to threaten to file a restraining order against him in order to get him to leave her alone," Doona said.

"James insisted that it was all just a misunderstanding, though," Hugh said. "He said that he still loves her, but he also thinks of her as his last connection to his brother. He also said something about wanting to make amends to her and to Larry for the years that they were estranged."

"You don't do that by sitting in your car outside of someone's house for hours on end," Doona said flatly.

"He claimed that was a misunderstanding, too," Bessie remembered. "Although he did admit that he'd sat in his car outside Amelia's home on several occasions. I'm not sure how that can be a misunderstanding."

"I think James needs to talk to a mental health professional," John said. "The question is, did he kill Larry?"

"I'd hate to think that he killed his own brother," Bessie said sadly.

"He's probably the person I'd put at the top of my list," Hugh said. "If only because he does seem somewhat – I don't know – unbalanced might be the right word."

"But was he unbalanced before Larry's death, or is that what triggered his mental health issues?" Doona asked.

"I really want to know what had changed," Bessie said. "Why had he and his brother started speaking again?"

"James said that he really regretted all of the years that he didn't speak to Larry," Doona said. "He said their relationship should have been more important than any woman who tried to come between them."

"To be fair, Amelia didn't know she was going to come between them. She didn't know they were related until after she'd fallen in love with Larry," Hugh said.

Doona nodded. "If I were James, once I'd found out that Amelia was cheating on Larry, I'd have been furious with her."

"And if she had been the victim, James probably would have been a suspect," John said. "But did James have any reason to kill Larry?"

"Maybe he just wanted Amelia back," Bessie suggested.

John sighed. "It's the best motive we've come up with for any of the suspects."

"But Larry was his brother," Hugh said. "And he and Amelia had been married for over ten years by that point. If he wanted Amelia back and he was prepared to kill Larry to get her, why did he wait so long?"

"Again, we need to know why the brothers were talking again," Bessie said. "Does anyone have any thoughts on Rosie?"

"I think the police need to investigate exactly what she's doing in her nursing career," Doona said. "She talked about taking on private clients, and Inspector Harrison made a note that several of her clients have left her considerable sums of money in their wills. He didn't say whether he was going to follow up on that or not. I think he should."

John nodded. "I found that worrying as well."

"She's also involved with two different men, neither of them seriously," Doona said.

"I have to say, while I didn't care for her as a person, I can't see her having any motive for Larry's murder," Bessie said. "I don't want to be horrible, but I can't see her caring enough about Larry to want him dead."

"If Larry had named her in his will, I might not agree," Doona said.

"Do we have a copy of Larry's will?" Bessie asked. "I don't remember seeing it."

"That's a good point," John said. "I don't remember seeing it, either. He may not have had a will, or it may have been so straightforward that the police didn't bother to include it."

"But it's worth asking Andrew about it," Bessie added, making a note.

"Herbert's interview almost made me laugh," Doona said. "After all their years of arguing, he said he actually still misses Larry."

"He did admit that the people who bought Larry's house repaired the fence before they moved in," John said. "Now Herbert has nothing to argue about with them."

"Did anyone else find it odd that Herbert asked out both

Amelia and Rosie in the weeks after Larry's death?" Bessie asked.

"I found it creepy, but not surprising," Doona said. "They're both attractive women, and Herbert struck me as lonely and maybe a bit desperate."

"Of course, they both turned him down," John said.

"Does the fact that he claims that he now misses Larry move him up or down the list of suspects?" Hugh asked.

"For me, neither," Bessie said. "But the fact that he tried to chat up the widow within days of Larry's death moves him up my list."

Doona nodded. "It was inappropriate."

"But by that time, everyone knew that Amelia had been cheating on Larry," Hugh said. "Maybe Herbert assumed that that meant that she wasn't all that sad that he'd died."

Bessie sighed. "And now we're back to Amelia. I still have my doubts about her."

CHAPTER 10

"Inspector Harrison reiterated in the most recent interviews that her alibi is unbreakable," Hugh said.

"Maybe he needs to try harder," Doona said.

Hugh nodded. "Maybe she killed him before she left for Auckland and then froze the body to help preserve it until just before her flight. If the body was frozen when she left, maybe the coroner got the time of death wrong."

"Is that possible?" Bessie asked.

Hugh shrugged. "I saw something similar in a movie once, but it was just a movie. I don't know enough about forensics to be certain if it could actually be done or not."

"I suppose we could ask Andrew to find out," Bessie said doubtfully.

"If she did kill Larry, then I'm surprised that Eric is still alive," Doona said. "She sounded very much as if she hated him because of the way that he treated her."

"Right after Larry's death, she insisted that they'd been going to leave their spouses and run away together," Bessie said. "She was even more definite about that plan in her most recent interview."

"Definite, and angry that it didn't happen," Doona added. "In her recent interview, she even suggested that they had dates in mind and firm plans as to where they were going to live and whatnot."

"She said something along the lines of hating all men now after the way that everyone has treated her since Larry's death," John said.

"I'm not sure that I blame her for that," Bessie said. "I would like to know why she's still working for Eric, though. It must be difficult working for someone that you dislike that much."

John nodded. "I'm not certain there's much else we can say about Amelia. Officially, she's not a suspect."

"Have they checked her financial records for any large payments to shadowy underworld figures?" Doona asked.

"Maybe Andrew should ask Inspector Harrison that question," Bessie said.

"We're putting together quite a list for Inspector Harrison," John said. "Are you going to share it with Andrew tonight?"

"He said he was going to come over once he got back from dinner in Douglas," Bessie said. "He should be here soon, actually."

"Does anyone have anything to add for now, then?" John asked.

"I'd like to talk about something else," Bessie said. "Ken is staying at The Margaret Hotel. Are any of you familiar with it?"

Hugh looked at John.

"I've been there," Hugh said eventually.

John nodded. "The hotel doesn't have the best reputation.

We probably have to send someone there about once a month on average."

Bessie frowned. "Has it always been that bad?"

"It has since I've been on the island," John told her. "The hotel is very isolated, really, and it's not in the best condition. It tends to attract a certain clientele, some of whom get themselves into trouble."

"What sort of trouble?" Bessie asked.

"Mostly, we get contacted with noise complaints," John replied. "Sometimes it will just be someone playing loud music in one of the rooms, but sometimes people will complain about guests arguing in the room next to theirs."

"And sometimes they're doing other noisy things," Hugh muttered.

Bessie felt herself blushing as Doona giggled.

"We've also had complaints about drug dealers using the hotel as a base of operations," John added. "We investigated that thoroughly, but we were unable to find any evidence that it was true."

"I should hope not," Bessie replied. "Hilary would never allow such a thing in her hotel."

"Hilary does her best," John said. "But she also goes home every night and leaves the hotel unattended. She can't control everything that happens there."

"She has a manager living at the hotel now," Bessie told him. "Maybe the number of complaints will go down."

"I didn't realise that. Who has she found for that job?" John asked.

"Her nephew, Harlan," Bessie replied. "Or, at least, he claims to be her nephew."

"Oh?" John raised an eyebrow.

"Hilary's eldest brother, Harold, studied religion at university and eventually became a Catholic priest.

According to Hilary, he fathered a child before he took his vows."

"And this child is now on the island?" Hugh asked.

Bessie nodded. "His name is Harlan Christian, or that's the name he's using, anyway. He's somewhere around fifty, and Hilary is letting him stay in one of the rooms at the hotel."

John flipped to a blank page in his notebook and made a few notes. "Has Hilary asked Harlan to take a DNA test?" he asked.

"No, and when Andrew suggested it, Hilary got upset and refused to consider the idea."

"Is that hotel all that Hilary owns?" was John's next question.

"It may be one of the last properties she owns," Bessie replied. "At one time, her family owned most of Lonan, but I believe Hilary has sold nearly all of the properties since her parents died. She may have a lot of money in the bank, or it all might have gone to pay her bills. I simply don't know."

"She doesn't live at the hotel?" Doona asked.

"Oh, no, she has a big house of her own," Bessie replied. "I'm certain I would have heard if she'd sold that."

John made another note. "I may have to go and have a word with Harlan Christian," he said. "It might be interesting to hear what he has to say."

"I really hope he is exactly who he claims to be," Bessie said. "I'd hate to think that he's lying to Hilary."

"Does he look anything like Hilary or her brother?" Doona asked.

Bessie frowned. "There may be a slight resemblance," she said after giving the question some thought. "But Harold was a fairly average-looking man. Harlan is much the same."

A knock on the door interrupted the conversation. Hugh opened it to let Andrew into the cottage.

"How was dinner in Douglas?" Bessie asked as John carried in another chair from the dining room.

"It was good. I enjoyed meeting Helen's friend, and we had excellent food," he replied. "I will admit that part of me really wanted to be here with you, working on the case, though."

"We didn't manage to solve it," Bessie told him.

"But we did come up with a long list of questions for Inspector Harrison," John added.

Andrew nodded. "I expected as much. Let me write them all down now, and I'll email them to him before I go to bed."

John flipped back through his notebook and then looked up at Andrew. "I think I jotted them all down. For a start, we want to ask Inspector Harrison to try harder to find out who told Janice about the affair."

Andrew nodded. "Definitely."

"While he's talking to Janice, we're interested in knowing more about her second husband as well," John continued. "Did they know each other before Janice and Eric separated?"

Andrew raised an eyebrow. "Are you suggesting that Janice was having an affair, too?"

"She admitted that they got married very quickly after her divorce was finalised, but she didn't actually say when she'd met the man," Bessie said. "We aren't accusing her of anything, we're just curious."

"Or nosy," Doona laughed. "It could be that we're just nosy."

"There's no such thing in a murder investigation," Andrew told her.

"We already talked about it, but I still want to know why James and Larry were talking again," Bessie said. "If James had stopped speaking to Larry because he was with Amelia, nothing had changed, so why start speaking again?"

"That's a question that feels very relevant to the murder," Andrew said. "Or maybe it just feels that way because James is always vague when questioned about the issue."

"There wasn't anything in the file about Larry's will," John said. "Who benefited financially from his death?"

"That's a good point. I should have noticed that omission," Andrew said.

"All of our other questions have to do with Amelia," John said. "We want her to be asked why she's still working for Eric after everything that's happened between them."

"Inspector Harrison should ask Eric why he's still working with her, too," Bessie said.

"She said something in her recent interview about struggling to find anything better," Andrew said. "But that really doesn't answer the question."

"The report didn't read as if she were asked that question directly," John said. "And I don't recall anything in Eric's interview about why he was still working with Amelia. He remarked several times that he'd ended his personal relationship with her, but didn't say much about their professional relationship."

"What else did you want Inspector Harrison to ask Amelia?" Andrew asked after making a few notes.

Hugh sighed. "Is there any way that she could have killed him before she left and then done something to – I don't know – cool the body or heat the body or something to make it seem as if he died while she was in Auckland?"

"That isn't my area of expertise, and I don't think it's Inspector Harrison's, either, but I can suggest to him that he speak to an expert on the subject. Does that mean you still think Amelia killed Larry?" Andrew asked.

"She certainly had the most obvious motive," Hugh replied.

"It may be more likely that she hired someone to kill him,"

Andrew said thoughtfully. "I know Inspector Harrison spent some time working on that idea before, but maybe he could give it another look. Was there anything else?"

"Isn't that enough?" Bessie asked.

Andrew laughed. "Inspector Harrison will probably think that it's plenty. I'll send this as soon as I get back to my cottage, but with the time difference, we may not have any answers for a few days."

"We're not meeting tomorrow. Let's hope you have answers by the next day," Hugh said.

"We can hope," Andrew said.

"We were actually talking about Hilary and Harlan just before you arrived," Bessie said as Andrew put his notebook in his pocket.

"Oh? Do I need to take more notes?" he asked.

Bessie shrugged. "I told the others the same things I'd already told you about Hilary and her family. I was mostly just expressing concern that Harlan is lying about his past to try to get his hands on Hilary's money."

Andrew nodded. "I've made a few enquiries, but I haven't heard anything back yet. I may hear something on that tomorrow."

"I should go," Hugh said after a large yawn. "It's getting late, and it's my turn to give Aalish her bath."

Bessie walked him to the door and gave him a hug before he left. As she turned back around, John and Doona were getting to their feet.

"We should go, too," John said. "I have to collect Amy from Ramsey before we go home."

"At least Thomas is at home already," Doona said.

"I keep thinking I'm going to miss them when they're both at uni," John said. "I know I will, actually, but I won't miss all of the extra driving."

Bessie hugged them both at the door and then watched as

115

they walked to John's car. She sighed as she shut the door behind them.

"They're so good together," she said. "But I think they're both afraid of getting married again."

"They both have failed marriages in their pasts. It's scary enough getting married when you're young and foolish. They both know exactly how difficult marriage can be, even if you really are deeply in love."

The pair chatted for a short while longer before Andrew looked at the clock and sighed.

"I need to go back and get some sleep," he said. "And before I do that, I need to send a long email to Inspector Harrison. What should we do tomorrow?"

"We've nothing we can do about the cold case until we hear back from Inspector Harrison. I was thinking that maybe we could go and talk to someone who knew Harold Christian."

"That's an interesting idea."

"I know someone who was at university with him, actually, but I don't know if they knew one another."

"I'm surprised you didn't mention him earlier."

Bessie frowned. "He isn't what I would call a friend," she said slowly. "Let's just say that he can be difficult."

"So you can't just ring him up and ask him about Harold."

"I wish I could. I'd much rather talk to him on the phone than in person, but I doubt very much that he'd talk to me at all over the phone. We'll have a slightly better chance in person."

"Where does he live?"

"He's in Port Erin. He lives in a care home there. He's nearly eighty. I'll ring a few friends in the morning, before we drive all the way down there, just in case he's moved again."

"Again?"

"He can be difficult. When he first sold his house and moved into a care home, he struggled to adapt to community living. I heard that he moved from place to place throughout the south of the island, trying to find the right fit. As I said, I'll ring a friend tomorrow and find out where he is now."

"Maybe he's in Douglas or Ramsey."

"I doubt that very much. Nigel loves the south of the island. He used to complain that the airport was too far north. I can't imagine him moving any farther north than Castletown."

"I can't promise that I'll be out of bed early, but if I am, I'll come and walk with you," Andrew said as he got to his feet. "Helen is probably smart enough to already be in bed, so she may join you, even if I don't."

"I'd be happy to walk with either or both of you. I'm happy on my own as well if neither of you get up early enough."

Bessie walked him to the door and then gave him a hug. Then she watched as he walked back to the nearest holiday cottage. As he let himself into the cottage, she shut and locked her door.

Ten minutes later, she snuggled under the duvet and shut her eyes tightly. *Maybe I should lie in a bit tomorrow,* was her last thought before she drifted off to sleep.

∽

"OR NOT," she said as she looked at the clock the next morning. It was two minutes past six and she felt wide awake and ready to start trying to find out more about Harold. She pushed back the duvet and climbed out of bed. She was standing in her kitchen, sipping a cup of tea, when someone knocked on her door.

"Helen, good morning," she greeted Andrew's daughter.

"Good morning," the fifty-something woman replied. "Have you already gone for your morning walk?"

"Not yet. I thought I'd have a cuppa first."

Helen laughed. "I did the same, but while I was drinking it, I kept an eye on the beach. I assumed I'd see you walking past at some point."

"I'm ready now," Bessie said, putting her teacup into the sink. "I just need to put on some shoes."

Five minutes later, the women were walking briskly across the sand.

"How are you today?" Bessie asked as they went.

"I'm good. Dad's health seems to be holding steady, which is better than I was expecting, actually. The books I brought with me to read while I was here have all been excellent. And I got to spend time with an old and dear friend last night, which was an unexpected bonus to this visit."

"I'm glad to hear that about your father."

"He's still going to need surgery, probably in the next few months, but obviously he wants to delay it for as long as possible. He's very concerned about how he's going to manage the cold case unit while he's recovering."

"Surely we can simply take a month or two off during his recovery. I can't imagine anyone will mind."

"Of course you can take a break, but Dad doesn't care for that idea. He's afraid if you skip a month or two that whatever magic is helping you solve every case might disappear."

Bessie sighed. "His health has to come first, though. I'll talk to him about it later."

"Please don't tell him I said anything. He doesn't ever want to talk about his health with me or anyone else."

"He's told me enough to worry me, so he should be expecting me to ask questions and express my concern."

"Thank you. I'm glad he has you in his life."

THE IRVING FILE

"I'm glad I have him as a friend, and I'm enjoying getting to know you as well."

They talked about Helen's family back in the UK as they strolled past Thie yn Traie and then even farther along the beach.

"We should probably turn around," Helen said eventually. "Dad is probably up. He said something about you needing to go to Port Erin today to talk to an old friend."

Bessie laughed. "Nigel Callister was never my friend, but I have known him for decades. I should say that I knew his family. His mother's family was from Laxey."

"Is there much to do in Port Erin? I thought I might ride down with you and enjoy Port Erin while you talk to your friend."

"There's a lovely beach and a few shops. The weather is fine, if you wanted a stroll along a different beach or to shop somewhere a bit different."

"It sounds as if it would be a perfect day to do either, or maybe both, of those things."

Bessie nodded. "I wish I could join you. I'm not looking forward to trying to speak to Nigel."

They stopped just outside of Helen's cottage.

"Dad and I will be over as soon as he's ready for the day," she told Bessie.

"I need to ring a friend and find out exactly where Nigel is living now. I'll see you shortly."

Inside her own cottage, Bessie flipped through her address book, trying to choose just the right person to ring. Eventually, she tossed a mental coin and selected someone.

"Joyce? It's Bessie Cubbon. How are you?"

They spent several minutes catching up on each other's lives before Bessie explained why she'd rung.

"I need to speak to Nigel Callister. Do you know where he's living now?" she asked.

Joyce laughed. "Why would you want to speak to him? I saw him last week and he's still as grumpy and impossible as ever."

"I have a few questions for him about someone he knew years ago."

"The good news is that his memory is still sharp as a tack. The bad news is that he's unlikely to share anything he remembers with anyone."

Bessie sighed. "I still want to try."

Joyce named a small care home near the beach in Port Erin. "He's as content there as he'll ever be anywhere. Lucy, the manager, takes good care of him. They seem to get along well, actually. It's an excellent home. One of my sister's close friends is there. I was visiting her when I saw Nigel last week. She can't say enough good about the home and about Lucy."

"It's good to know that such places exist."

"Yes, but you'll never move out of your cottage, will you?" Joyce asked with a laugh. "I used to feel that way about my little cottage here, but in the last year or so I've started to consider other options. I'm getting rather tired of dealing with leaky roofs and broken cookers."

"I'm quite content in my little cottage on the beach. I can't imagine living anywhere else."

They talked for a short while longer, only ending the conversation when Andrew and Helen knocked on Bessie's door.

"Ready for Port Erin?" Andrew asked after they'd exchanged greetings.

"I know where to find Nigel," Bessie replied. "I'm hoping by the time we get to Port Erin I'll have worked out a way to get him to tell me what I want to know."

CHAPTER 11

"I'm looking forward to spending some time in Port Erin," Helen said as they made their way south. "I love Laxey Beach, but a change of scenery is always good."

"I can't imagine that the beach in Port Erin will feel any different to Laxey Beach," Andrew replied.

"I think it feels very different," Bessie told him.

"You did say there are some shops within walking distance, didn't you?" Helen asked Bessie.

She nodded. "And a few cafés and coffee shops as well. If you get tired of walking on the beach, you'll have plenty of other options."

"Excellent. Just ring my mobile when you're done, but feel free to take your time," Helen said.

"I don't imagine we'll be long at all," Bessie replied. "I don't expect the man we're going to see will want to speak to us."

Andrew stopped the car in the car park next to the beach.

"It already feels very different to Laxey Beach," Helen said as she gathered up her handbag and her jacket. "I don't know that I need to worry about the shops. I may just walk forever in one direction or the other."

As Helen began her slow stroll towards the water, Bessie gave Andrew directions to the care home where Nigel was living. It took them only a few minutes to drive there. Andrew parked in the small adjacent car park and looked at Bessie.

"Have you worked out what you're going to say to Nigel?" he asked.

She shook her head. "I've decided to wait and see what sort of reception I get. Nigel is nothing if not unpredictable."

"Maybe he'll be feeling friendly today."

Bessie chuckled. "We can hope."

They got out of the car and walked to the door. A bell chimed quietly as Andrew pulled it open. By the time they'd entered the small foyer, a woman in a nurse's uniform was waiting for them.

"Good morning," she said brightly. "How can we help you today?"

"I'm hoping to visit Nigel Callister," Bessie replied.

The woman nodded. "Is Mr. Callister expecting you?"

"No, not at all," Bessie said. "I wanted to ask him a few questions about someone that he used to know years ago."

"Mr. Callister isn't always in the mood for visitors, but I'll be more than happy to tell him you're here and see what he says. I'll just need your names."

"I'm Elizabeth Cubbon, and this is my friend, Andrew Cheatham."

"And you are both friends of Mr. Callister?"

"I'm sorry to say that I haven't spoken to him in years, but I have known him for a long time," Bessie replied.

"I'm afraid I've never met the man," Andrew added. "But Bessie has told me about him."

THE IRVING FILE

The woman raised an eyebrow. "Has she now? Let me go and see if Mr. Callister is awake and interested in having any visitors, then."

She turned around and unlocked the door behind her before disappearing through it. Andrew walked over and sat down on the small couch that was against the wall. After a moment, Bessie joined him.

"This is a lovely old house," Andrew said.

"This much of it is lovely, anyway. I really hope we get to see more of it."

Andrew chuckled. "Whatever happens, we have lots of other options. The best thing we could do is persuade Hilary to have DNA tests run, of course."

"And she seems adamant that she won't do that."

"I'm not certain if that means that she's satisfied that he's actually her nephew, or if it means she has her doubts and she doesn't want them confirmed," Andrew said.

Bessie frowned. "Why wouldn't she want them confirmed? Surely she doesn't want to be scammed out of her family's fortune."

"Maybe she wants to believe that Harlan is who he claims to be, even if she doubts it's possible. You did say that she didn't have any other family left. Now she has family."

"If I were her…" Bessie began. She stopped as the door at the back of the room opened again.

"Mr. Callister will speak to you in the conservatory," the nurse told them. "If you'd care to follow me?"

Bessie and Andrew stood up and crossed to the door. The woman opened it and then held it open for them to walk through before she shut it and then checked that it was securely locked.

"We have to be very mindful of the safety of our residents," she told them. "But the conservatory is just down here."

They walked down a short corridor, past a number of shut doors, before they reached the very end. A small sign identified their destination. The nurse pulled the door open and then motioned for them to go inside.

"Mr. Callister will be with you shortly," she said before stepping back.

The door slowly shut by itself.

Bessie looked around the small, glass-walled conservatory. It overlooked a small garden at the back of the property. "Someone is a keen gardener," Bessie said as she looked out through the windows.

"Indeed. The gardens are lovely." Andrew said as he sat down in one of the chairs.

"I'm amazed at how many different colours of flowers are included. I'm also surprised that somehow they don't clash or even seem to compete with one another, in spite of their numbers," Bessie replied as she took the seat next to his.

The pair chatted about the flowers and plants for several minutes before the door opened again. The man who joined them was almost entirely bald. His eyes were brown and mostly hidden behind thick glasses. He walked slowly but steadily into the room, stopping near the centre.

"Elizabeth Cubbon," he said in a gravelly voice. "I thought you'd be dead by now. You certainly look a good deal older than you did the last time I saw you."

Bessie inhaled slowly, counting to ten before she replied. "That's hardly surprising, as I don't believe I've seen you in more than twenty years," she replied eventually.

Nigel shrugged. "Twenty years or last week, it hardly matters. We were never friends."

"Speaking of friends, this is Andrew Cheatham. He's a friend of mine from across."

Nigel glanced at Andrew and then looked back at Bessie.

"Since you're here, I'm going to guess that someone has died and you're poking your nose into the investigation. That seems to be all that you do these days."

"No one has died," Bessie snapped. She inhaled again as Andrew squeezed her hand. "And it's been several months since I was involved in any murder investigations on the island." Bessie chose her words carefully. She couldn't talk about the cold case unit, after all.

Nigel shrugged. "So what are you investigating? Gloria, the nurse, said you had some questions for me."

"I do have a few questions, but I'm not exactly investigating anything," Bessie replied. "I heard something about someone the other day that surprised me, and I wanted to try to find out more, that's all."

"I should sit down," Nigel said before he walked over to the chair next to Bessie's and sat down heavily. "Because I'm tired, not because I have any intention of turning this into a long conversation. I'm not especially interested in helping you pry into other people's lives."

"I'm not trying to pry," Bessie protested. "I'm trying to protect someone."

"Of course you are," Nigel said. "By snooping around and asking questions about them behind their backs."

Bessie flushed. "Maybe we should go," she said to Andrew.

"But things are just getting interesting," Nigel said mockingly. "Maybe I should guess who you want to discuss. I don't know all that many people on the island, and most of the people that I do know don't care for me. That rather limits the list, really. Were you telling the truth about it not being a murder investigation?"

"It's not a murder investigation," Bessie replied.

"Are you investigating my Uncle Edward? Truthfully, it's

about time someone investigated the man. He's always had a lot more money than he should have, considering that he's a window cleaner. If you ask me, I think he's been making quite a lot of extra cash by not talking about what he's seen through the windows he cleans, if you know what I mean."

"You think he's blackmailing his customers?" Andrew asked.

Nigel shrugged. "I wouldn't have put it that way, but maybe."

"What's Edward's surname?" was Andrew's next question.

Nigel shook his head. "I'm not getting my favourite uncle into trouble, or my least favourite uncle, either. He's one of those, but I'll not tell you which. So it isn't Uncle Edward. Interesting. What about my sister-in-law, Wilma? I'd be delighted to hear that she's being investigated for something. I'd be even happier if you tell me that she's going to be arrested soon."

"What do you think she might be doing that might lead to her being arrested?" Andrew asked.

"I wish I knew. I've often thought about trying to frame her for something, just to get rid of her, but I've never managed to come up with a proper plan."

"Wilma is your brother's wife?" Bessie asked.

Nigel nodded. "We've never cared for one another. I've no idea what my brother ever saw in her. She was passably pretty when she was younger, but that was decades ago and they're still together."

"Maybe they love one another," Bessie said.

"I suppose that's one possibility. And from your reaction, I guess you aren't here because of her. Who else could it be? Let me think."

"I can just tell you," Bessie offered.

"Bah, what fun would that be?" Nigel replied. He glanced

at his watch. "I'm just killing time until lunch. My telly broke last week, and I haven't replaced it yet. Telly in the morning is rubbish, anyway, but I used to watch it, regardless. I've not much else to do all day, really."

"What sorts of books do you enjoy? I could probably recommend a few titles in just about any genre," Bessie offered.

Nigel laughed. "I don't especially enjoy reading. I'd much rather watch people on the telly, racing around and doing things, than sit in a chair with a book, trying to imagine the pretend people doing pretend things."

"That's where we differ," Bessie told him. "I quite enjoy spending time lost in a good book."

"I plan to go into Douglas tomorrow to get a new telly. If my telly were working, I wouldn't have bothered to talk to you today." Nigel glanced at his watch. "Lunch is still an hour away, so I can keep guessing why you're here. Maybe it's something to do with that horrible woman who runs the care home where I used to live. If she's turned up dead, you'll have more suspects than you can manage."

"No one is dead," Bessie replied tightly.

"Well, now, after all the murders you've poked your nose into, you must have lots of ideas on how to kill someone and not get caught. If you want to do me a favour, go and get rid of Mrs. Lemke for me. I'd even pay you for the effort."

Bessie wasn't certain whether she wanted to laugh or shout at the man. She took another deep breath while Andrew chuckled softly.

"Bessie isn't a killer for hire," he told Nigel.

"She could be, though, and no one would ever suspect her. Not now, not after all the cases she's solved."

"How well do you remember Harold Christian?" Bessie asked.

Nigel stared at her for a minute. "You're going to have to give me more than that to go on," he said. "I know at least three Harold Christians, but I'm pretty certain they're all dead."

Bessie nodded. "It's a small island, with not enough surnames to go around."

Nigel laughed. "And a shortage of Christian names as well, really. Kids today seem to have more imagination than we did forty or fifty years ago. I see all sorts of odd names in the local paper now. Odd Christian names, that is. There are quite a lot of comeovers with odd surnames, too, I suppose."

"I'm curious about the Harold Christian who went to university with you," Bessie told him. "The man from Lonan."

"Ah, Father Harold," Nigel laughed. "We didn't know each other before we went to uni, but we met within the first few days. Everyone was going around asking everyone else where they were from, of course, and we were both pleased to meet someone else from the island. It turned out that was all that we had in common, though."

"Oh?" Bessie asked, trying not to sound disappointed.

"Yeah, Harold was already thinking of becoming a priest. He was Catholic, or he was thinking about becoming Catholic. I forget which, but it didn't much matter. What mattered was that he wasn't interested in going out and meeting women, and that was just about all I wanted to do."

Bessie sighed. "So you didn't get to know him well?"

"We talked whenever we saw each other on campus, but we never went out of our way to spend time together. We did sail back and forth together a few times, more by luck than design, but when we both ended up on the same ferry, we usually sat together and talked."

"Did Harold ever mention having a girlfriend?" Bessie asked.

Nigel laughed. "Father Harold? He stayed as far away from women as he possibly could. He said something once about doing everything he could to avoid temptation. It meant we often struggled to find things to talk about on the ferry, of course, because women were my primary interest in those days."

"I was afraid of that," Bessie said, almost to herself.

"Why?" Nigel demanded. "What's happened?"

Bessie hesitated and then sighed. It wasn't as if Hilary had asked her to keep Harlan a secret. "I have a friend staying at The Margaret Hotel," she explained. "Hilary still owns it, but she has a man staying there who claims to be her nephew, Harold's son."

Nigel stared at her for a moment. "Harold's son? Impossible." He sat back in his seat and then tipped his head back.

Bessie watched as he breathed in and out for a full minute. Then she looked over at Andrew and shrugged.

"Thank you for your time," Andrew said.

"Shush," Nigel snapped without opening his eyes.

Bessie looked at her watch, keeping an eye on the second hand as it swept around the dial eleven times before Nigel opened his eyes and sat back up.

"It's only just very remotely possible," he said. "I have only the vaguest of recollections of the conversation, but there was something. We were coming back to the island for Christmas during our last year of study, and Harold was even quieter than normal. I was too busy bragging about my latest conquests to pay much attention, but I do remember finally asking him if he was okay. He said something about realising that the path he'd chosen was going to be more difficult than he'd imagined. I laughed and told him that he should sleep with a few dozen women before he took his vows, and he muttered something about not wanting dozens, just one. I must have pressed him for more information, but I can't remember anything more of the conversation."

Bessie sighed. "So he may have found himself a girlfriend, or at least a woman in whom he was interested."

"And he may have been intimate with her before he joined the priesthood," Nigel added. "I only saw him once after that ferry journey, and that was in the spring. I had already lined up a job back on the island for after I'd finished my degree. When I told Harold about the job, he was happy for me. Then he told me that he'd actually decided to go to a seminary and become a priest. In hindsight, I should have asked him about the girl, but I'd mostly forgotten about the conversation by that point, really."

"I don't suppose you want to go to Laxey and meet Harlan," Bessie said.

"I wouldn't mind seeing Hilary again, actually," Nigel replied. "I met her once, when she was waiting for her brother at the Sea Terminal on one of our journeys back to the island. Once I moved back, we went out a few times. She was beautiful and smart, too smart for me. She ended things after about a week."

"I'm not just being nosy," Bessie told him. "I'm concerned that the man is simply pretending to be Harold's son in order to con Hilary out of everything she owns."

"Surely they can just run a DNA test. I see that on telly all the time, men getting told they aren't the fathers of the children they thought were theirs."

"Hilary doesn't want to have DNA testing done," Bessie replied.

Nigel shrugged. "In that case, you should probably stay out of it. You've given her your advice. Now it's up to her to decide what she wants to do with it."

Bessie pressed her lips together. "I just hate the idea of a con man profiting from his con," she said eventually.

"Knowing Hilary, she's put him to work. He'll end up earning every penny he gets from her," Nigel replied. "Unless he kills her, of course, but then you'll be there, ready to solve the murder, won't you?"

"Thank you for your time," Bessie said, getting to her feet.

Nigel laughed. "I'm sure I've been much more helpful than you were expecting. You should be grateful to my broken telly, really."

"I am," Bessie replied flatly.

Nigel was still chuckling to himself as Bessie and Andrew left the room. They made their way back towards the entrance. The nurse they'd spoken to when they'd arrived stopped them as they reached the foyer.

"I hope Mr. Callister was able to help," she told Bessie.

"He was much more pleasant than I was expecting him to be," she admitted.

The nurse laughed. "Lucy, the owner here, keeps telling him to be nicer to people. She'll be delighted to hear that she's having an effect."

Bessie and Andrew walked back outside and got into his car.

"That was frustrating," Bessie said as they headed back towards the beach.

"We learned that it's possible that Harold had a girlfriend at some point in his university days."

"Yes, but even if he did, it seems unlikely that he was intimate with her."

"What we've learned does seem to tie in with what Hilary said about Harold not knowing about the baby. If he had known, I would have expected him to insist on marrying the woman," Andrew said. "Perhaps we should try to find out more about Harlan's mother."

Bessie sighed. "Or maybe we need to stay out of it and let Hilary investigate if she decides she wants to know more."

"That's always an option."

Andrew parked the car near the beach.

"For now, let's stroll on the beach, find my daughter, and then get tea and biscuits somewhere," he suggested.

"That sounds wonderful," Bessie replied.

CHAPTER 12

"I hope you had a productive morning," Helen said when they found her walking on the beach.

"It was more productive than I'd been expecting it to be," Bessie told her before she told Helen everything that they'd learned from Nigel.

"It sounds as if it's possible that Harold had a girlfriend at some point, then," Helen said when Bessie was finished. "But I find it difficult to believe that a man who was planning to become a priest would abandon his pregnant girlfriend."

Bessie nodded. "Hilary did say that Cassandra, Harlan's mother, never told him about the baby. I can't help but be curious about her."

"I may have some answers to the questions I sent my friend about Harlan," Andrew told her. "That should tell us more about his mother."

The trio made their way to the nearest coffee shop and enjoyed tea and biscuits while they talked about movies and actors. After they were finished, they headed back towards Laxey.

"I don't think I want any lunch," Helen said, patting her tummy. "I may have eaten a few too many biscuits."

"I shall have a very small sandwich," Bessie said. "We all should eat something healthy to tide us over until time for dinner."

"What are we doing for dinner?" Andrew asked.

"Maybe we could try that restaurant that you always talk about," Helen suggested. "The one that does the small plates with three or four different things on them for both dinner and pudding."

"That's a good idea, especially for a day when we're only having a light lunch," Bessie replied. "You need to be very hungry when you eat at Dan's restaurant."

Andrew nodded. "I may not even have a sandwich. I'm fairly certain I ate enough biscuits to get me through until dinner."

"But you'll have a small sandwich to make me happy," Helen said. "Because I worry about your diet."

Andrew chuckled. "I didn't actually have that many biscuits. I'll have a sandwich," he agreed.

When they reached Laxey, he parked outside of Bessie's cottage.

"I need to go and check my emails. I'm hoping to have replies from both New Zealand and London," he said. "And I'll have a sandwich," he told Helen.

"I think I'll curl up with a book," Helen said. "After I have some lunch, of course."

"Either or both of you are welcome to visit after you've eaten," Bessie told them. "I shall be having my sandwich and then going back through the cold case file until we have to leave for Onchan."

With their plans made for later in the day, Bessie headed inside Treoghe Bwaane. She made a sandwich and sliced an apple into easy-to-eat pieces and then settled down at the table with her case file. An hour later, her telephone rang, making her jump.

"Hello?"

"Aunt Bessie? It's Andy Caine. How are you?"

"I'm fine. How are you?"

"I'm good, thanks. I was just wondering if you were busy tomorrow."

"I have an appointment in the afternoon, but my morning is free," Bessie replied.

"Would you be willing to come with me to look at a house?"

"Of course."

"Thanks. As ever, I'm sure you'll know the whole story behind the property."

"What's the address? While I'm happy to go with you to look at the property, I can also just tell you if I know anything about it."

Andy chuckled. "I know you can, but I'd rather have you there, if you don't mind. It's always helpful to have a second opinion on things."

"And I'm always happy to share my opinion," Bessie replied with a laugh.

"As for the address, it's Christian Cottage, Laxey."

Bessie inhaled sharply. "Do you have the particulars of the property?"

"I do, and let me tell you, it isn't a cottage. According to the estate agent's listing, it has twelve bedrooms and six bathrooms, three of which are ensuite to bedrooms. It's a much larger house than I need, of course, but I was wondering about applying for planning permission to turn part of the building into a restaurant."

"That's an idea," Bessie said, her mind racing. *Why had Hilary Christian put her house up for sale? Was it possible that Harlan was trying to sell the house behind her back?*

"I'll collect you at half nine, and I'll tell the estate agent to expect us shortly after that. According to the directions, the house is about halfway between Laxey and Lonan."

"Yes, that's right. I've been there once before, but it was a long time ago. You'll need the directions because it isn't easy to find."

"That may not be ideal for a restaurant, then," Andy laughed. "But we'll see what we find tomorrow."

"Would you mind terribly if my friend Andrew came along?"

"Of course not. The more the merrier."

"He may have other plans, but if he doesn't, he may want to see the house, too. He recently met the owner, Hilary."

"You know the owner? Of course you know the owner. I can't imagine why I was surprised."

Bessie laughed. "I don't actually know everyone in Laxey, but I do know the owner of Christian Cottage. She also owns a hotel in Lonan. Andrew has a friend visiting the island this month and he's staying at The Margaret Hotel, which is Hilary's hotel."

"And Hilary owns Christian Cottage?"

"Sorry, did I not say that? Yes, Hilary Christian owns the cottage that is actually a large mansion and the hotel that is, well, more what Americans would call a motel than a proper hotel."

"Is she selling that, too? Maybe it would be a better location for the restaurant."

"I don't think she's selling the hotel, but I also didn't know that she was selling her house, so she may be selling the hotel, too."

"I'll have to ask my estate agent when I see her tomorrow," Andy said. "I'll see you around half nine."

Bessie put the phone down and then frowned at it. She reached for it again, intending to ring Hilary, but stopped herself before she actually picked up the receiver. "Wait and see what tomorrow brings," she told herself.

She went back to the case file, but found it difficult to concentrate. When Helen and Andrew came to find her to head to Onchan for dinner, she was sitting on the large rock behind her cottage, staring at the sea.

"Is everything okay?" Andrew asked as he sat down next to her and took her hand.

"Everything is fine," Bessie replied. "Except I'm going with Andy Caine to look at a house tomorrow. Not just any house – Hilary Christian's house."

Andrew frowned. "I've learned a few things about Harlan. Let's talk about them on the drive."

The pair walked to Andrew's car, where Helen was waiting. Once inside, Andrew pointed the car in the direction of Onchan.

"Hilary has put her house on the market, then," Andrew said after a minute.

"Andy was sent a listing for it, anyway," Bessie replied. "That isn't proof that Hilary has put it on the market, though."

Andrew glanced over at her. "Do you suspect that Harlan is trying to sell it behind her back?"

"That may be one possibility," Bessie replied with a sigh. "I truly don't know what to think. That house has been in the family for decades. Hilary's grandfather had it built to his specifications. I suppose I never imagined that she'd sell it."

"Is it a large house?" Helen asked.

"When it was built, it had fourteen bedrooms," Bessie told her. "Andy said that, according to the listing, it has twelve bedrooms and six bathrooms. I imagine some of the bedrooms have been turned into ensuites for other bedrooms. Ensuites are common now, but they weren't when the house was built."

"And Hilary lives there alone?" was Helen's next question.

Bessie nodded. "She's lived there alone for several years now."

"I can't say I blame her for wanting to sell," Helen replied. "Even if she has help, that's a lot of house to maintain, and it must feel huge and empty when she's the only one there."

"But it's been her home for her entire life," Bessie countered.

"Do you think Andy would mind if I came along on the house tour?" Andrew asked as he pulled the car into the car park for the restaurant.

"I already asked, and he said you're more than welcome to join us," Bessie replied.

"Can I come, too?" Helen asked.

Bessie laughed. "He did say 'the more the merrier,' so why not?"

Inside the busy restaurant, Bessie was happy to see Carol Jenkins, Dan's wife, who was seating people when they arrived.

"How are you?" she asked as Carol hugged her.

"I'm doing really well. The baby is getting big, and we're talking about maybe trying for one more, but that's a conversation for another day," Carol replied. "For now, let me find you a table."

She showed them to a table in the corner.

"This is lovely," Bessie said as they all sat down. "What is Dan doing for the sample plate tonight?"

"It's a celebration of the number two," Carol replied wryly. "It's all about things that are better in twos, or at least things that can be eaten in twos. You'll get two cheese raviolis in tomato sauce, two small chicken and vegetable skewers, two tiny battered fish fillets, and two baby Yorkshire puddings filled with roast beef and gravy."

"Wow, that sounds as if it will be a lot of food," Helen said.

"We do have a standard menu, if you'd prefer something else," Carol told her.

Helen laughed. "Oh, goodness, no. I want the sample plate. I just hope I can save room for pudding."

"More twos?" Bessie asked.

Carol nodded. "Two tiny lemon tarts, a pair of chocolate truffles, two small brownie squares, and two small scoops of ice cream. We have a choice of flavours for the ice cream."

"Maybe I should just have one of each of the things on the plate," Bessie said.

"We can do that, if that's what you want," Carol told her. "The servings are actually quite small, though. Just one of each thing might not be enough for you. We can always put anything left over into a box for you to take home. We can do the same with pudding if you can't manage it here."

"I'll have the sample plate, then," Bessie said. "And I want to see pictures of the baby when you have time to share some."

Carol laughed. "I have an entire album of photos that I can leave with you. You can look at as many or as few pictures as you want and then give the book back to me."

"Perfect," Bessie said.

She and Helen looked through the photos while they chatted and waited for their food to arrive.

"Everything is so good," Helen said after she'd tried a few bites of each of the options. "I thought I'd have a favourite, but I don't think I do."

"I like the chicken skewers," Bessie said.

"I prefer the fish," Andrew told them. "But I'm mostly looking forward to pudding."

"I can't believe I ate that much," Helen groaned as they walked outside a short while later. "I should have been sensible, too."

Bessie patted her small box of puddings. "These will go nicely with a cuppa when we get back to my cottage."

"I'm sure they will, but I simply couldn't wait," Helen said.

They were still talking about the food when Andrew parked outside of Bessie's cottage.

"I'll just come and check things over," he said as they all got out of the car.

Bessie didn't bother to argue. Instead, she opened her door and then let Andrew and Helen into the cottage first. As Andrew walked around the first floor, Bessie put the kettle on.

"Tea?" she asked when he came back into the kitchen.

"Yes, please. We never did talk about what my friend learned about Harlan."

"Tell me everything," Bessie said as she prepared tea for everyone.

"Am I okay to stay?" Helen asked.

Andrew nodded. As Helen sat down at the table, Bessie piled a handful of biscuits onto a plate. Then she put the contents of her box from the restaurant onto a small plate for herself and offered a plate to Andrew.

"I'll just eat my puddings out of my box," he said. "Unless you'd rather I used a plate."

Bessie hesitated and then shrugged. "I suppose it doesn't matter," she said before she sat down and picked up a lemon tart.

"Those were really good," Helen said as she reached for a biscuit. "I preferred the brownies, but those were very good."

Bessie took a bite as Andrew opened his box.

"So, my friend in London took a very quick look at Harlan," he began after his first bite. "He didn't find much, but what he did find seems to match up with what we've been told so far. Harlan's mother was at the same university at the same time as Harold, but she quit after her second year. Six months later, she gave birth to Harlan, who was about a month early, by her doctor's reckoning."

"Did your friend find any proof that she actually knew Harold?" Bessie asked.

Andrew shook his head. "As I said, he only took a quick look, mostly through public records. In order to dig further, he'd have to be a good deal less discreet."

Bessie sighed. "Let's see how tomorrow goes. I'm curious what the estate agent is going to say about the house. Hopefully, he or she will know why it's on the market."

They chatted about Hilary and Harlan while they finished their tea before Andrew and Helen headed back to their cottage. Bessie spent another hour going back through the case file before she headed to bed.

"Of course, Andrew didn't tell me whether he'd heard anything from New Zealand or not," she said with a sigh as she combed her hair. "I hope Inspector Harrison has found answers to all of our questions and that the answers will help us solve the case."

With that thought in mind, she crawled into bed and shut her eyes tightly.

Bessie's internal alarm woke her just before six the next morning. After a shower and some breakfast, she took a long walk on the beach, trying to ignore her worries about both Hilary and Larry Irving.

"I feel as if we've been neglecting poor Larry for the past two days," she told Andrew when he and Helen knocked on her door just after nine.

"We haven't talked about him much, but that's because we've been waiting for answers to our questions. I have some of those now, and I may have more before we meet this afternoon. For now, let's focus on Hilary," he replied.

"But I'm being paid to try to solve Larry's murder," Bessie countered.

"But you aren't being paid to think about the case all the time. We'll spend the entire afternoon talking about Larry, I promise."

Bessie nodded as Andy's car pulled into the parking area outside her cottage. A few minutes later, the foursome were heading towards Lonan in Andy's sporty car.

"I asked my mum about the property," Andy said as he drove. "She said she thought she'd heard something about the family, but she couldn't remember much."

Bessie laughed. "Your mother never had time for skeet. She was always working." She gave Andy a quick history of the family on the short drive.

"It's left here," Andrew said from the back of the car. Andy had given him the listing from the estate agent, asking Andrew to provide directions as needed.

"Here?" Andy asked, stopping and staring at what appeared to be not much more than a path through the tall grass on the side of the road.

"I'm not certain your car can manage that," Andrew said.

A horn honked behind them. Andy pulled forward and to the side of the road. "That's my estate agent," he told Bessie.

The car stopped next to them, and the driver motioned for Bessie to put her window down while she did the same.

"I know it doesn't look as if it's a road, but I promise it gets better just past the trees," the woman said. "I'll go first, and you can follow me."

She put her car into reverse before anyone could reply. Bessie watched as she turned off the road and into the grass. As she slowly drove away, Andy backed up and followed.

"At least she wasn't lying about it getting better," Andy

said as they drove through a row of tall trees. Just past them, the path turned into a paved road that appeared wide enough for two cars. They followed the road for a short distance, until the house appeared in front of them.

"Wow," Helen said. "It's huge and it's gorgeous."

Bessie nodded. "I remembered it being lovely, but it's even nicer than I recalled."

"I thought it was overpriced when I first saw the listing," Andy said. "Now I think it's underpriced."

"You haven't seen the inside yet," Bessie said. "They may not have had anything done to it in decades."

"I'm not sure I'd care," Andy said as he parked the car. "I'm a little bit in love with it already."

An hour later, they'd had the full tour.

"As you can see, the property could do with some modernising, but it's in excellent condition," the estate agent said as they returned to the huge foyer at the entrance.

"It is lovely," Andy agreed. "But it's much larger than what I need, really."

"You could turn the dining room and kitchen into your restaurant," the woman replied. "And then you could turn one of the bedrooms on the first floor into a small private kitchen for your own use."

Andy nodded. "I was thinking that, actually, but I'm not certain I want to live above my restaurant. I have a lot to think about."

"I never know what to advise with properties of this sort," she replied. "Often, because of their size and price, they'll sit on the market for months or even years, but sometimes they'll generate a lot of interest and go very quickly."

"Why is the owner selling?" Bessie asked.

"She's decided to find herself a more manageable property," was the reply. "She lives here alone, and this is far too much house for a woman in her seventies to manage."

Bessie looked around and nodded. "It is a very large house, but I never expected Hilary to sell her family home."

"You know the owner, then? When I spoke to her, I got the impression that she didn't truly want to sell, but she also doesn't need a house of this size. Her nephew was with her, and he encouraged her to put it on the market, at least. He told her that she could always turn down offers if she changed her mind, but that he had no interest in ever living here."

Bessie frowned. "So he talked her into putting it on the market."

"I think it was more a case of him encouraging her to do what she already knew she ought to do," the estate agent countered.

"Maybe we should have a word with Hilary," Andrew suggested.

"Would you all mind terribly if I took another walk through the house?" Andy asked. "I want to try imagining it as home."

Bessie and Helen sat together in the large sitting room while Andy took another look around. Andrew used the time to ask the estate agent about other properties that were available on the island.

"I've been thinking of moving here," he explained. "But I haven't found the right property yet."

They were still chatting when Andy reappeared.

"I'm going to have to think about it," he said with a sigh. "And on the drive back to Bessie's, I want to know what you all thought."

They chatted about the house all the way back to Bessie's and then over lunch. Andy made omelets for everyone while they talked.

"Thank you all for coming with me and sharing your thoughts," Andy said as Helen took care of the washing-up. "I still don't know what I want to do, but I appreciate your input."

"If you rang the estate agent to make an offer and she told you that someone else had already bought the place, how would you feel?" Bessie asked.

Andy frowned. "That's a tough one. There was a lot that I loved about the house, but it needs a lot of work, too." He sighed. "I'm going to sleep on it. What I really want to do is ask Elizabeth for her opinion, but, well, that's impossible, isn't it?"

Bessie swallowed a dozen different replies before she spoke. "It would be an excellent place for someone to hold weddings and other special events," she said. "Perhaps Elizabeth would be interested in investing with you so that she could use the property for her business."

"I was thinking that exact same thing, but I don't really want to go there," Andy sighed. "I've messed things up with Elizabeth rather badly."

"A property like that one doesn't come on the market very often," Bessie pointed out. "Maybe you should ring Elizabeth and suggest that she take a look. That's the sort of thing a friend would do."

"I'll think about it," Andy promised as he hugged Bessie tightly. "Thanks again for your help this morning."

As Bessie shut the door behind Andy, Andrew grinned at her.

"I need to check my emails one more time, but then we need to devote our afternoon to Larry," he told her.

CHAPTER 13

"After the meeting, maybe we should go and visit Hilary," Bessie said as she and Andrew made their way towards Ramsey.

"We could, or we could wait and see what else we can learn about Harlan and his mother before you speak to her again."

"That might be smarter, but at the moment we have an excuse to be at the hotel. Once Ken goes home, we'll lose that."

"That's very true, and Ken is flying back to London tomorrow."

"He is? But we haven't solved the case yet."

Andrew chuckled. "Remember, he isn't here to work with us on the case, even though he is doing some of that. He's here to learn how the cold case unit functions. He's already seen as much as he needs to see. He was thinking of flying back yesterday, but he decided to stay until we had the answers to some of our questions, instead."

"I'm anxious to get some answers, too."

"We're nearly at the Seaview."

Five minutes later, Andrew pulled his car into the hotel's car park. They were halfway to the door when someone shouted Bessie's name. She frowned as she turned around.

"Dan? Hello," she said unenthusiastically.

Dan Ross, an investigative journalist with the local newspaper, smiled at Bessie. "Here for another meeting?" he asked. "I've heard that there's another Scotland Yard police inspector on the island this month. Apparently, he's staying in Lonan at The Margaret Hotel. I don't suppose you know anything about him?"

Bessie shrugged. "No comment," she said.

Dan chuckled. "Of course, of course, but that tells me much more than you want me to know. It tells me that you know the man and don't want to talk about him."

"On the contrary," Bessie countered. "I would give you the same response whether I knew the man or not. I'm simply not interested in sharing anything I know with you."

"You know the owner of The Margaret Hotel, though, don't you? Hattie something or other."

Bessie bit her tongue. She inhaled slowly and then sighed. "Again, no comment."

"Inspector Cheatham, do you have anything to add to Bessie's statement?" Dan asked Andrew.

Andrew laughed. "'No comment' isn't a statement by any stretch of the imagination, but I'm not interested in telling you anything, either. Now I'm afraid we have to go. We're expected elsewhere."

"Yes, of course, you have a meeting. You and several other police inspectors and Bessie. That seems very odd to me," Dan replied. "Why include Bessie?"

"I quite enjoyed the last James Bond film," Andrew said. "Did you?"

Dan frowned. "I suppose so. They're all much of a muchness, really, but they're a decent diversion for an hour or two."

"And potentially quite educational," Andrew suggested.

"Educational?" Dan looked at Bessie and then back at Andrew. "Is that a clue? Are you telling me something I don't know? Is there a hint in the latest Bond movie that would tell me what you're doing on the island? I can't even remember what happened in the latest Bond film."

"Perhaps you should see it again," Andrew said before taking Bessie's arm. The pair walked away as quickly as they could.

"I'll do that," Dan shouted after them. "And then we'll talk again."

Bessie waited until they were on the lift to speak. "What was that all about?" she asked. "What happened in the latest Bond film?"

Andrew shrugged. "I haven't seen a Bond film in years. It just popped into my head as something that might distract Dan for a few minutes."

Bessie was still chuckling softly when they reached the penthouse conference room. Hugh was already at the table, a full plate of food in front of him.

"Someone cancelled a birthday party for this afternoon," he told them as they walked into the room. "Jasper gave us some of the food that had already been prepared."

"I'm sorry I had lunch," Bessie said as she took a look at what was available.

"We didn't eat all that much," Andrew said as he began to fill a plate.

"I'm torn between finger sandwiches, the miscellaneous finger foods, and the trays full of puddings," Bessie replied as she picked up a plate of her own. She filled it with a little bit of everything and then sat down next to Andrew at the table.

The rest of the group arrived together a short while later.

Once they all had food and drinks in front of them, Andrew cleared his throat.

"We've had some answers," he said. "Some of them may well generate more questions, but let's work through them one at a time."

"So who told Janice about the affair?" Hugh asked.

Andrew sighed. "That was one that Inspector Harrison couldn't answer. He went back and spoke to Janice again, but she insisted that the caller hadn't given a name and that she didn't recognise the voice. When Inspector Harrison questioned why she'd believed a total stranger, she told him that she'd already had some suspicions, but she'd been ignoring them because she didn't want to believe that Eric would ever cheat on her."

"And she didn't do anything to confirm what the caller said before she flew to Auckland to confront her husband?" Ken asked.

"She said that the caller knew enough to convince her – that after their conversation, she knew that he was telling the truth."

"He?" Bessie asked.

Andrew frowned and looked down at his notes. "Inspector Harrison has written it as he, but that may not be what Janice said."

"Was she asked to describe the voice?" Hugh asked.

"She said it was a normal voice, maybe male, but she couldn't be certain," Andrew replied after checking his notes.

"So did she actually refer to the caller as 'he' or not?" Bessie asked.

"I'll ask Inspector Harrison. He should be able to check the recording that he made of the interview."

"Of course, many people use the word he when they mean he or she," Ken said. "It may not mean anything."

149

"I still think she knew the caller," Bessie said. "And I think his or her identity could be important to the case."

Andrew flipped to a blank page and made a note before turning back to where he'd been previously. "Inspector Harrison also asked Janice about her second husband," he said.

"The one she married only a short while after her divorce was finalised," Doona said.

"She insisted that they met only after she and Eric had separated, but that she'd known almost instantly that he was the man she wanted to be with for the rest of her life," Andrew told them.

"That surprises me, considering how badly her first marriage had imploded," Ken said.

"But she wanted more children," Doona said. "It's possible she started actively looking for a man who wanted children as soon as she knew her marriage was over."

"Or even before," Bessie suggested. "Maybe she didn't meet her second husband before she found out about the affair, but maybe she was already looking for a new man. Perhaps she exaggerated her outrage and anger when she did find out, even though she'd already been planning to leave."

"Maybe Inspector Harrison should ask her that," Hugh said.

Andrew made another note. "I'm not certain it makes much difference," he said. "But the inspector needs to question her again anyway."

"We wanted to know why James and Larry were speaking again," John said.

Andrew nodded. "Inspector Harrison spoke to James but found him less than cooperative."

"Oh? That's interesting," Bessie said.

"Surely he wants his brother's killer found," Doona said.

"He told the inspector that talking about Larry was difficult for him. He said that he was still struggling with guilt over not having spoken to Larry for so many years and frustration that Larry was murdered before they'd had a chance to properly reconcile."

"But he wouldn't tell Inspector Harrison why they'd started speaking again?" Hugh asked.

"He said he couldn't remember the details, but that there wasn't any significant event or anything. He said it was probably as simple as them bumping into one another somewhere and then simply starting to speak."

"I don't believe it," Bessie said. "They hadn't spoken in over ten years. He must remember what happened to change things, even if it was just a chance meeting somewhere."

Andrew nodded. "I'm inclined to agree with you."

"So we think both Janice and James are lying," Harry said. "How well do they know one another?"

"I don't know that they do know one another," Andrew replied.

"That may be something else they should be asked," John suggested.

Andrew nodded. "It's an interesting question."

"I wonder if James knew about the affair," Bessie said thoughtfully. "I'm not sure how he would have felt if he'd found out that his beloved Amelia was having an affair, though."

"Even if he didn't know at the time, he found out after Larry's murder, and from all accounts, he's still in love with Amelia," Hugh replied. "So maybe he did know, and maybe he rang Janice and shared that information with her."

"That's definitely one possibility," Andrew said. "Although I'm not certain what James had to gain from telling Janice about the affair."

"Maybe he suspected that Eric would end things with Amelia if the truth came out," Doona said. "Maybe James found out about the affair and that was why he'd started talking to Larry again. Maybe he wanted to be there when Larry found out about the affair, so he could persuade Larry to divorce Amelia over it."

"And then he'd be there to help poor Amelia after both men in her life ended things with her," Bessie said.

"Too bad someone killed Larry before James could put his plan into place," Hugh said.

"Unless killing Larry became part of the plan," Bessie said softly. "What if James told Larry about the affair and Larry didn't care? What if Larry said that he would do anything he could to keep Amelia, in spite of the affair? What if Larry just laughed and said that he and Amelia had an open relationship? Maybe James felt that he had to get rid of Larry in order to win Amelia back."

John sighed. "That all sounds sadly plausible," he said.

Andrew nodded. "Let's go through the rest of the questions and then we'll talk more about James. We asked what was in Larry's will. It was pretty straightforward. Most of the estate went to Amelia, with a few specific bequests to others, including a pocket watch that went to James."

"A pocket watch?" Hugh echoed. "Does anyone still use pocket watches?"

"This one had belonged to their father," Andrew explained. "Larry had inherited it when their father died, but as he didn't have any children of his own, he left it to James in his will."

"And that's all that James received?" Bessie asked.

"It is. The recipients of the other various items aren't on our short list of suspects. Inspector Harrison has given me a complete list, along with brief biographies of each person, but none of them were ever considered suspects in the case. The items that were left ranged in value from one hundred to about four hundred pounds."

"So nothing significant," Charles said. "Unless something in the collection had sentimental value for someone."

"I suppose it's possible, but Inspector Harrison spoke to all of the beneficiaries and ruled them all out. I'll let you all have a copy of the interviews with each of them. I read them last night and didn't find anything of interest in them," Andrew replied.

"I think the rest of our questions had to do with Amelia," Bessie said. "I'm sure Inspector Harrison didn't appreciate that we questioned her alibi."

"He was polite, but insistent that there was no way that she did it," Andrew replied. "He told me that he'd checked and rechecked her alibi, and it's as watertight as these things can be. She was in Auckland well before the man's death, and he found enough people who'd spent time with her there to be certain that she didn't fly back and forth to kill him."

"And the body hadn't been tampered with, frozen or heated or anything," Hugh asked.

"They're certain that Larry died in the bed where he was found," Andrew replied. "And they're confident that they have an accurate time of death. None of that proves that Amelia wasn't involved in some other way, but she definitely wasn't there when Larry died."

Hugh nodded. "So she paid for someone to kill him."

"That's a possibility, but her bank accounts were gone over by an expert, and she couldn't find any unexplained expenses in Amelia's accounts or Larry's."

Doona winced. "Imagine using your husband's account to pay to have him murdered."

"There's no evidence to suggest that she did any such thing," Andrew said.

"So where does that leave us?" Bessie asked.

Andrew nodded at his notebook. "I have a list of follow-up questions. Does anyone have any more to add?"

"I did think that Amelia was the key to the whole case," Bessie said. "She was married to the victim, after all. But now I'm starting to become more curious about James."

"He would have been smarter to just make up a story about Larry ringing him out of the blue and wanting to talk," Hugh said. "Larry isn't around to dispute it, and we'd probably be paying him less attention if we didn't think he'd lied to the police."

"And Janice could have said that it was Larry who rang her," Doona added. "It would make perfect sense for the angry husband to ring the wronged wife, wouldn't it?"

"And maybe it was Larry who rang her," Andrew said. "But maybe she didn't want to admit that after Larry turned up dead."

"I suppose I can see her point," Doona replied.

"Inspector Harrison also noted that he did some more checking into Oscar, following our recommendation. He said he has a lot more investigating to do, but it appears as if Oscar may be involved in something criminal where he's currently working."

"If he is, maybe he was doing something similar when he was working with Larry. And maybe Larry found out and Oscar needed to silence him," Doona said.

"The inspector is going to keep digging into Oscar's past and present activities. Even if he didn't kill Larry, it appears as if he might be going to prison soon, anyway," Andrew said. "And while the inspector is doing that, he needs to speak to Janice again. Maybe, when he points out that she referred to the caller as 'he,' she'll confess all."

"Maybe the inspector should start by asking her how well she knows James," Bessie suggested.

Andrew nodded. "And we want to know if she was looking for a new man before she found out about the affair as well."

"That sounds a bit cold, but we did talk before about how Eric hadn't wanted any more children, but she had," Bessie said. "We should have had the inspector ask her about that when he spoke to her recently."

"We had so many questions for him, I'm not surprised that we missed a few," Charles said.

"I'll ask him now," Andrew told them. "But I'm more curious about her relationship with James."

"I think you should have him ask Amelia about James," Bessie said. "I know you mentioned that she was considering getting a restraining order against him. Is he still bothering her? And does she think he might have killed Larry?"

Andrew made a few notes and then looked around the table. "Anything else?"

"The more we talk about him, the more I'm suspicious of James," Doona said.

Hugh nodded. "I think he got back in contact with his brother so that he could kill him."

"But why wait so long?" John asked.

"Maybe the affair was what drove him over the edge," Ken said. "As Bessie said earlier, maybe James found out and told Larry, but Larry didn't care, so James killed him."

Bessie frowned. "It's all rather horrible."

"But plausible," John replied.

"I'll send all of our questions to Inspector Harrison as soon as I get back to Laxey," Andrew told them. "We'll meet again the day after tomorrow to go over the answers, assuming we have any."

"Sadly, I'll have to miss that," Ken said. "I'm flying back to London tomorrow morning."

"It was a pleasure meeting you. Good luck with your cold case unit," John said.

That seemed to be everyone's cue to start packing up their things. A short while later, Bessie found herself alone with Ken and Andrew after everyone else had said their good-byes and disappeared.

"Would you mind terribly if we followed you back to Lonan?" Andrew asked Ken as the threesome headed for the door.

"Not at all, but do you mind if I ask why?" Ken replied.

"Bessie wants to talk to Hilary again," Andrew explained.

"Have there been any more late-night visitors?" Bessie asked.

Ken shook his head. "It's been very quiet at The Margaret Hotel – almost too quiet. I live in London, after all."

In the car park, Andrew waited to start his engine until Ken was driving away. "We don't want to get there before he does," he told Bessie. "He's our excuse for visiting, after all."

"I'm not certain I need an excuse," Bessie replied. "I may just tell Hilary that I'm there to try to help her."

"Remember that she believes Harlan."

"I don't know that she does. I suspect she simply wants to believe Harlan. She's all alone in the world. I'm sure the idea of having someone, anyone, is very appealing to her."

"I'm sure you can understand the appeal."

"Yes, of course. If I didn't have family in the US, I'd probably be starting to wonder what to do with my estate when I pass away. As it is, I've no shortage of relatives to whom I can leave my cottage, but obviously Hilary's situation is quite different."

Bessie thought about the situation for the rest of the short drive to the hotel.

CHAPTER 14

Andrew pulled into the hotel's car park a short while later. Ken's car was parked in front of his room, and Andrew parked next to it.

"What now?" Andrew asked.

"I'm going to see if Hilary is here," Bessie replied.

"Do you want me to come with you?"

Bessie thought for a moment and then shook her head. "It's probably best if you don't."

"I'll go and chat with Ken, then."

They got out of the car. Andrew walked to Ken's door and knocked while Bessie headed for the office. She knocked and then opened the door.

"Hello," Harlan said from behind the counter. "Something wrong?"

Bessie shook her head. "I wanted a word with Hilary."

"She's not here."

Bessie sighed. "Do you know where she is?"

Harlan nodded. "Yes."

Swallowing another sigh, Bessie forced herself to smile. "Is she going to be here later today?"

DIANA XARISSA

"She should be."

"Soon?"

Harlan looked at the clock. "Yes."

Before Bessie could ask any more questions, she heard a car coming down the road towards the hotel. She watched as it rolled to a stop right in front of the office door. After a moment, Hilary opened the door and stepped out of the car.

"Bessie," she said, nodding.

"Hilary," Bessie replied. "I was hoping to have a word with you."

Hilary shut the car door and then walked slowly towards Bessie. "Is someone dead?"

"No, of course not. I was wondering about your house, that's all."

Hilary raised an eyebrow. "My house?" She sighed. "Come in and we'll talk."

Bessie followed Hilary into the office.

"Did I miss anything?" Hilary asked Harlan as she walked across the room.

He nodded. "A booking for Christmas week."

Hilary frowned. "Are you sure you want to have guests during Christmas week?"

"I'll be here. Why not?" Harlan replied.

Hilary shrugged. "It's up to you. I'm going to take Bessie in the back for a chat. Shout if you need me."

Harlan nodded and then watched as Bessie followed Hilary through the door behind the counter. It opened into a tiny room that was barely wide enough for the small couch that was pushed up against the back wall. There was a small refrigerator and a sink against one of the side walls. A table with a kettle and a few coffee cups was flat against the wall on the other side.

"Have a seat," Hilary said, gesturing towards the couch.

Bessie sat down and tried to get comfortable on the thinly

padded seat. Hilary filled the kettle and then switched it on. While it was heating, she dumped a packet of biscuits onto a plate.

"Tea?" she asked Bessie once the kettle had boiled.

"I'd love some," Bessie replied.

Hilary made the tea and then set up a small folding table in front of Bessie. She put their teacups and the plate of biscuits on the table and then sat down next to Bessie.

"Isn't this nice?" she asked as she picked up a biscuit.

"It is, thank you," Bessie replied.

"There isn't anything better than tea and biscuits to go along with nosy questions."

Bessie flushed. "I came because I am concerned. If you don't want to talk about your house, we can talk about something else."

Hilary sighed. "How did you discover it was on the market?"

"My friend, Andy Caine, is looking for a property. He asked me to accompany him when he went to see a house, and when he told me the particulars, I immediately realised it was your house."

"Have you been around it, then?"

Bessie nodded. "We went this morning."

"What did your friend think? Is he likely to want to buy it?"

"He's considering it. It's a huge house, though. It may be more than he needs."

"Andy Caine? Isn't he the man who inherited the Teare family fortune? He can buy the house and fill it with staff, from what I heard."

"He did inherit the Teare fortune, but as I understand it, there wasn't as much money there as everyone had always imagined."

DIANA XARISSA

"He should have stuck with Elizabeth Quayle. She could probably buy my house with her pocket money."

Bessie chuckled. "I don't think the Quayles have as much money as that."

Hilary shrugged. "It doesn't really matter. I just want someone to buy it."

"Why? I mean, it's been your home for a very long time."

"What did you think of it when you went around it today?"

"I thought it was lovely, very large, but beautiful, with amazing views."

"I will miss the views, I suppose, but I won't miss the size. I live alone. I certainly don't need twelve bedrooms. Of course, I don't use eleven of them, but they still have to be cleaned from time to time, and they're still just there, sitting empty, reminding me that I'm all alone in the world."

"I'm sorry," Bessie said.

"It would be different if I had staff who lived with me, but that's a huge expense, and besides, it's completely unnecessary. I can manage quite happily on my own, mostly. I do my own cooking and shopping, at least. I do have a woman who comes in and cleans for me twice a week, but she doesn't have time to clean the entire property. She cleans the rooms that I use and then, once a year, I have her and some of her friends come and clean the entire house from top to bottom."

"What a good idea."

"If your friend does buy the property, I'll give him the woman's name. She's very good, and she knows the house and all of its unique characteristics."

"I'm sure he'd appreciate that."

"He wants to have a restaurant, doesn't he? Maybe he could turn the ground floor into a restaurant and then live on the upper floors. It's far too large a house for even a family, really. I did think that someone might want to buy it and turn it into a bed and breakfast."

"It would need more ensuite facilities."

Hilary nodded. "I had two of the bedrooms turned into ensuites for three different bedrooms. There are plenty of other rooms that could be converted as well."

"When did you have the work done?"

"About ten years ago. I was actually thinking about using the house as a bed and breakfast myself, but then I decided that I didn't want strangers staying in my house."

"I can understand that."

Hilary sighed. "I don't even allow Harlan to stay with me, and he's family."

Bessie chose her words carefully. "He seems happy enough staying here."

"He is. He's made some friends, and they probably come and see Harlan at all hours of the day and night, which they wouldn't be able to do if he were staying with me. I do hope they haven't disturbed your friend."

"He said something about late-night guests one night, but I believe it was only the one time."

"Harlan probably didn't think to tell his friends that the hotel had a guest." Hilary made a face. "Sadly, it's quite unusual for us to have guests, aside from TT fortnight and during the Grand Prix."

"You are a bit out of the way out here."

Hilary laughed. "That isn't the only reason why we don't get guests. The hotel is old and run-down. I'm quite aware of its shortcomings. Harlan has lots of ideas for improving it. I suggested that we try to sell it, but he wouldn't hear of it. It's a piece of family history, the history of a family he's only just discovered is his, or so he said."

"And you're quite certain he's who he claims to be?"

"Quite."

Bessie nodded. "Where will you go once your house is sold?"

"I can always stay here for a bit. I may do that, actually, until I'm ready to, well, make other arrangements."

"I think, if I owned a hotel, that I'd go and stay in it at least once a month," Bessie said thoughtfully.

"But maybe not if it were this hotel," Hilary suggested. "As I said, I'm well aware of its shortcomings. But if Harlan gets his way, he's going to change all of that. He's already ordered new mattresses for all of the rooms, and he's been testing out pillows and bedding as well. He gets furniture catalogues and rug samples in the post nearly every day. By this time next year, all of the rooms will probably be completely redone."

"That all sounds expensive."

"I've plenty of money in the bank. Last year, I sold the last of the family businesses, aside from this hotel. Once I sell the house, this hotel will be the only property I still own. It really ought to be as nice as it possibly can be."

"And you aren't worried about Harlan stealing any of the money from you?" Bessie blurted out.

Hilary took a sip of her tea and then slowly nibbled her way through a biscuit.

"I'm sorry," Bessie said to break the awkward silence. "I don't have to tell you that over the past few years, I've seen a lot of horrible things that people do to one another. That's made me worry more than ever about my friends."

"I do understand your concern. If I were in your place, I'd probably feel the same way," Hilary told her. "I'm simply trying to decide how much I should share with you."

"Please, don't share anything with me," Bessie said quickly. "We can talk about the weather or local politics for a few minutes and then I'll go quietly."

Hilary laughed. "I do appreciate your concern. As I said, I might feel the same if I were in your position. But you need to understand that I don't have anyone else. Until Harlan arrived on the island, I was planning to leave my entire estate to charity. I hadn't decided which charity, though, and it was starting to become a real concern."

"I can imagine. There are so many good causes out there."

"And some organisations that appear to be good causes, but aren't. You know what I mean."

Bessie nodded. "Sadly, I do."

"But then everything changed. Harlan is here, and now I know exactly what to do with my money. My nephew is going to inherit everything I own. If things go to plan, that will just be this hotel, which is more than he ever imagined owning before he met me."

"So he timed his arrival perfectly," Bessie said, trying not to sound as suspicious of that timing as she felt.

"More perfectly than you know." Hilary took a deep breath. "I'm dying, rather more quickly than most. I still feel quite well, but my doctor reckons I've not much more than six months left. I don't expect to see another Christmas, but I've never been overly fond of Christmas anyway."

"I'm sorry."

Hilary shrugged. "Everyone has to go eventually. I've had a good life. We had more than enough money, a large house, and several family businesses. If I could do it all again, I think I might marry the man who asked me when I was nineteen, but, at the time, I thought I could do better. As it happens, I was wrong."

"I'm sorry about that, too."

"Regrets are mostly a waste of time and energy, but I do wonder sometimes where I would be now if I had married Nick. We would probably have had children. I never could imagine myself as a mother, but such things were inevitable in those days."

Bessie nodded. "I sometimes wonder where I would be if I'd married the man I loved."

"I remember hearing something about that. He was Australian, wasn't he?"

Bessie blushed. "I did have a friendship with a man who was from the island but had moved to Australia. We met while he was visiting family here. That isn't the man to whom I was referring, though."

"Oh?"

"I met Matthew Saunders in the US when I was only seventeen. When my parents decided to move back to the island, they insisted that I come with them, even though I wanted to stay behind and marry Matthew."

Hilary grinned. "This all sounds vaguely familiar. I must have heard the story at some point."

"I believe everyone on the island has heard the story," Bessie told her.

"Am I right that he died when his ship sank when he was on his way to the island to get you?"

"Not exactly. He died on the voyage, but the ship didn't sink. He simply fell ill and passed away."

"Now I'm the one who is sorry," Hilary said.

"It was a long time ago."

"But you still wonder what might have been."

"Just sometimes. Of course, I still have family in the US. My sister married her boyfriend, and she stayed in Ohio with him. They eventually had ten children."

"Ten? My goodness. Maybe it's better that I never married."

Bessie nodded. "I'm fairly certain that I couldn't have managed ten children."

"But at least you have someone to whom you can leave your estate."

"I do."

"And I didn't, not until Harlan turned up unexpectedly."

"And it doesn't worry you that he turned up on your doorstep at just the right time?"

Hilary stared at her for a moment and then sighed. "It doesn't worry me, because I simply don't care."

"You don't care?"

"I don't care if he's lying. I don't care if he's trying to con me out of my estate. I don't care if he's planning to murder me in my sleep one of these days."

Bessie gasped. "But..."

Hilary held up a hand. "There are no buts. I don't expect him to murder me in my sleep, but if that's what he's planning, well, he's only bringing my death forward by a matter of weeks or months. He's well aware of my prognosis. He was with me when the doctor gave me the news."

"And you don't care if he isn't really Harold's son?"

"I've been alone for a very long time. And then, suddenly, six months ago, I found out I have a nephew. Whether Harlan truly is my nephew or not, he's been acting the part for the past six months. He came to the island and moved in here. He's been managing the hotel, and doing a good job of it, too. He's not asked me for a single penny. I pay him for the job he's doing here, but that's all."

"But he must know that he's going to inherit everything when you die."

"I've told him that it's all going to charity. He said that was fine with him. He has a small house in Bolton that he's planning to return to once I'm gone. He's only stayed on the island this long because he knows I don't have much time left. I'm his only family, too, you see."

"Will he stay on the island once he actually inherits the hotel?"

Hilary shrugged. "Who knows? The good thing is, I'll be dead, so I don't have to worry about what happens to the hotel then. My father wanted it to stay in the family. I'm doing my best to make certain that happens. Harlan can do what he wants with it once I'm gone."

"I'm sorry that I questioned his intentions," Bessie said.

"I do understand that you were trying to protect me," Hilary replied. "I know there are a lot of people out there who try to take advantage of older folks, especially women living on their own. If I thought I had a lot more years left, I'd probably be more concerned about Harlan's intentions. As it is, I'm just happy to have his company in my final days."

"Maybe you'll prove the doctors wrong and live for another dozen years."

"I appreciate the thought, but I don't expect that to happen. Harlan's birthday is in November. I'm very much hoping to still be around for that, since I missed all of his previous birthdays."

"What do you think Harold would think of his son?"

"I think he'd be amazed and proud, but also disappointed that Cassandra never told him. He loved his life as a priest, but there was always a part of him that wondered what his life might have been if he'd made other choices. One of the things he always felt that he'd missed out on was being a father."

"Cassandra should have told him."

Hilary nodded. "I wish she had. I would have loved having a nephew to spoil. And maybe they would have had more children. I would have been an amazing aunt."

Before Bessie could reply, someone knocked on the door.

"Come in," Hilary shouted.

Harlan opened the door and looked in at them. "Sorry, but someone is looking for Bessie Cubbon."

"That will be Andrew," Bessie said, getting to her feet. "I rather lost track of time."

Hilary nodded. "We've been talking for ages."

THE IRVING FILE

"I enjoyed it, though," Bessie replied before she headed back into the main room.

Andrew was standing behind the counter. He smiled at her as she emerged from the back room. "I'm sorry to interrupt, but I was starting to worry."

"And you have better things to do than just sit around while Bessie and I talk about what we'd do differently if we could do our lives over," Hilary said with a laugh.

"I'm sorry," Bessie said. "We were having tea and biscuits, and I forgot that you were here, waiting for me."

"If you want more time, it's fine," Andrew replied. "I can come back for you later."

"No, I need to get back to Laxey. We've been out for hours," Bessie told him.

Bessie was nearly at the door when Hilary spoke again.

"Bessie, wait. I want to give you something," she said before she turned around and disappeared into the back room again.

Andrew gave Bessie a curious look. Bessie shrugged. When Hilary emerged again, she was holding an envelope.

"Here," she said, handing it to Bessie.

Bessie looked at it and then at Hilary. "It's stamped 'private and confidential.'"

"Yup. But I'm giving it to you. You can do what you want with it."

"What is it?" Bessie asked.

"When Harlan first arrived, my advocate insisted that we needed to have a DNA test done so that we could be certain that Harlan truly was Harold's son. It wasn't that he didn't trust Harlan as much as he wasn't certain that Cassandra was telling the truth in her letters."

"My mother wouldn't have lied," Harlan said quietly.

Hilary nodded. "Anyway, my advocate sent everything away somewhere and then got the results. He wanted me to open the envelope in his office so that he could see the results, but by the time they'd arrived, I'd already realised that I didn't care what they revealed. I'm more than happy to acknowledge Harlan as my nephew. I was going to burn the letter the next time I used the fireplace at the house, but it's June, so I haven't done it yet."

"Do you want me to burn it, then?" Bessie asked, feeling confused.

"I don't care what you do with it. Burn it. Read it first and then burn it. Or read it and then frame it and put it on the wall in your kitchen. As I understand it, there shouldn't be anything in the letter that identifies anyone. It should just say that person A is or is not related to person B."

Bessie turned the sealed envelope over in her hands. "You should open it," she told Hilary.

"I don't want to know what it says," Hilary replied. "It doesn't matter to me, but I thought you might want to know."

"Take the letter," Andrew said softly. "You don't have to open it."

"But if you do, don't tell me what it says," Hilary added.

Bessie nodded and then slid the envelope into her handbag.

"I hope to see you again soon," she told Hilary. She nodded at Harlan and then followed Andrew to his car.

CHAPTER 15

"I really don't want the letter," Bessie said to Andrew as he started the car.

"Why don't you tell me everything that was said?" he suggested.

Bessie spent the journey to her house repeating what she could remember of her conversation with Hilary. They sat in Andrew's car, outside of Bessie's cottage, while she finished the story.

"I suppose I can see Hilary's point," Andrew said when she was done. "If she has only a few months to live and she's been alone for a long time, I can see why she doesn't care if Harlan is actually Harold's son or not."

"But she actually had a DNA test run. I couldn't possibly have the results and not check them."

"Maybe she's afraid she'd be disappointed."

Bessie sighed. "I'm going to put the letter in my fire."

"Before or after you read it?"

"I wish I knew."

Andrew followed her to her door. "Let's go somewhere nice for dinner tonight," he suggested. "Our cold case seems to simply be going around in circles. There isn't anything we can do now until I hear back from Inspector Harrison."

"Or you and Helen can come here, and I'll cook," Bessie suggested. "I could make cottage pie."

Andrew grinned at her. "Now that you've said that, that's all that sounds good. Are you quite certain you don't mind cooking?"

"Not at all. And I think I could do with a quiet night at home."

They agreed on a time, and then Andrew headed back to his cottage to send another email to Inspector Harrison. Bessie went inside Treoghe Bwaane. She put her handbag on the counter and then took out the letter.

"What should I do with you?" she asked. She held the envelope up to the light, wondering if she would be able to see anything through it. Sadly, all she could see was the outline of the piece of paper inside.

"I need to prepare dinner," she said loudly. "I don't have time to worry about this right now." After a moment's thought, she carried the envelope up to her small office and locked it inside a desk drawer. Then she went back downstairs and started on the cottage pie.

Andrew and Helen arrived right on time.

"I brought pudding," Andrew announced, putting a bakery box on the counter.

"Where did you get that?" Bessie asked.

"Helen and I went for a drive, just for a change of scenery," Andrew replied.

"Dad was driving me crazy," Helen said. "He's waiting for an email that he knows he won't get for hours and hours."

Andrew nodded. "I've had an interesting message from New Zealand, but I need to wait for the follow-up message before I say anything. But that message probably won't arrive until tomorrow."

"Do we need to have a meeting tomorrow, then?" Bessie asked.

"We probably should, actually. It sounds as if there has been a break in the case, and I'd rather tell you all about it in person than send emails to everyone."

"Do you want to meet at the Seaview, or would it be easier just to meet somewhere here in Laxey?" Bessie asked.

"We can meet in my cottage," Andrew said. "Charles and Harry can walk there, and it's closer for the others than Ramsey. If we set the meeting for two, I should definitely have something to tell everyone."

"And Ken will have missed it all by less than a few hours," Bessie said.

"I may ring him and suggest he change his flight," Andrew said thoughtfully. "But let's have dinner first."

They ate quickly, enjoying the cottage pie and the chocolate fairy cakes that Andrew had brought. As soon as they were done, Andrew started ringing people, setting up the meeting for the next day. Bessie helped by ringing Doona and Hugh on his behalf.

"That's everyone," she told him after he'd spoken to Charles, Harry, and Ken. "Doona and John will definitely be here. Hugh needs to rearrange something but should be able to be here."

"Ken changed his return flight to the last one of the evening, so he'll be here, and so will Charles and Harry," Andrew told her. "Now we can all sit around and wait for that email."

Bessie sighed. "Waiting isn't easy."

"We could walk on the beach," Helen suggested.

The trio walked at a leisurely pace along the sand. As they passed the holiday cottages, Harry shouted hello at them from his cottage.

"I do hope we've solved another case," he said to Andrew as he joined them at the water's edge.

"I'm not certain what's happened," Andrew replied. "The email that I received was incredibly vague, but it suggested that there had been some sort of breakthrough."

"Maybe someone confessed," Helen said. "Maybe being questioned again after all these years finally pushed someone's guilt to the breaking point and he or she confessed all."

"That's one possibility, and it isn't unheard of," Harry said. He told them stories about unexpected confessions as they walked as far as the new houses.

"It doesn't look as if Hugh and Grace are at home," Bessie said, feeling slightly disappointed. "It's been a while since I've seen Aalish, and she seems to grow dramatically between my visits."

"Children do in their first few years. Things slow down a bit once they get to school age," Andrew told her.

"Was school very different in America?" Helen asked Bessie.

The little group chatted about their school experiences as they walked back towards Bessie's cottage. Bessie was surprised and pleased that even Harry offered a few anecdotes from his past.

"I'll see you all tomorrow at two, then," he said when they reached his cottage.

A few minutes later, they were behind Andrew's cottage.

"I'm going up to bed," Helen said. "If I wake up in time, I may join you for your morning walk," she told Bessie.

Andrew walked Bessie to her door. "Do you want me to come in and sit with you while you open those DNA test results?" he asked.

"You're curious about what they say, aren't you?"

"Of course I am. I assume you are as well."

Bessie shrugged. "I'm curious, but I'm also worried that I

might be disappointed in them. I truly want Harlan to be Harold's son."

"Would you rather give me the envelope? I can keep it somewhere safe for you until you decide what you want to do with it."

"It's quite safe where it is," Bessie assured him. "If I give it to you, you'll just open it."

Andrew laughed. "I won't open it if you'd rather I didn't, but I would be awfully tempted, really."

"Let's worry about that tomorrow, after we've heard what's happened in New Zealand."

"I think that's a good plan."

Bessie locked the door behind Andrew and then switched the ringer off on her telephone. At the top of the stairs, she hesitated and then deliberately shut the door to her office.

"Worry about it tomorrow," she muttered to herself as she walked into her bedroom.

∽

AT FIVE MINUTES PAST SIX, Bessie opened her eyes. The envelope in her desk was the first thought that crossed her mind. "We might have a break in the cold case," she told herself as she got out of bed. "That should be what you are thinking about today."

After her shower, she thought briefly about Matthew as she dusted herself with the powder that smelled of the roses that he'd given her very early in their relationship.

"You'd open the envelope, wouldn't you?" she asked, wondering what the man would actually say if he were sitting next to her in some shared space.

"Except there wouldn't be any envelope, because we were going to go back to America to live," she added. "And now I'm talking to a ghost."

She made herself some toast, adding a thick layer of honey to sweeten her mood. Once that was gone, she headed out for a brisk walk. When she got back to Treoghe Bwaane, she felt as if she could almost hear the letter calling to her from its drawer on the first floor.

"I can't hear you," she said loudly. "And I don't want to open you, either."

Helen came over a short while later. "Dad is sitting at his computer, pressing send and receive every five minutes," she told Bessie. "I'm going to take the hire car and go into Ramsey for some shopping. I promised Dad that I'd get food for lunch today, in case he's still waiting, and some biscuits and cakes for your meeting this afternoon as well."

"That's very kind of you."

"Anything is better than sitting around watching Dad twitch every time he gets another email advertising amazing summer holidays or expert double glazing."

Bessie laughed. "And people wonder why I don't have a computer."

"If you aren't doing anything else, you're more than welcome to come into Ramsey with me," Helen said.

"I can always use an extra trip to the shops," Bessie replied, feeling at least as eager to get away from the letter as she was to go shopping.

It was nearly time for lunch when the women got back to Laxey. Helen helped Bessie carry her shopping inside and then gave her a hug.

"Do you want to come over to our cottage for lunch?" she asked.

Bessie thought for a moment and then shook her head. "If your father hasn't had his email yet, he'll be impossible company. If he has had it, I'm afraid I might just demand that he tell me everything he's learned. That isn't fair to the rest of the unit, though."

THE IRVING FILE

"I'll see you around two, then. I've told Dad that I'll help make drinks for everyone, and then I'll take myself off for a long walk on the beach. He's promised to text me when you're done."

"I can give you a key to my cottage," Bessie offered. "Then, if you get tired of walking, you'll have somewhere to go."

"That's very kind of you, but Harry has already made the same offer, and his cottage has a telly."

Bessie laughed. "I suppose I can't compete with that."

"There is a programme that I was hoping to watch later. Otherwise I'd probably take you up on your generous offer and spend the time going through your bookshelves."

"You can do that any time."

"I may take you up on that."

Bessie had a light lunch. She knew that Helen had purchased several packets of biscuits and cake slices for the meeting, so she didn't want to eat too much. It was still a few minutes before two when she made her way across the sand to Andrew's cottage.

"Hello," Andrew greeted her with a big smile.

"You've had your email, then," Bessie guessed.

He shook his head and then laughed. "I haven't had an email, but Inspector Harrison rang me about an hour ago. I've been bursting to tell someone ever since."

"But you're going to insist on waiting until the others arrive to tell me, aren't you?"

Andrew hesitated. Before he could reply, someone knocked on the door. Andrew let Harry and Charles into the cottage. John and Doona weren't far behind. Ken and Hugh arrived as Helen was pouring tea for everyone.

"I'd better start walking," she said as Andrew shut the door behind Hugh.

"Here's my key," Harry said, handing it to her. "Let yourself in and watch whatever you want. I'll knock when I get back."

"Thanks," Helen replied as she headed for the door.

As soon as the door shut behind her, everyone looked expectantly at Andrew.

"Do you all have tea and biscuits?" he asked, looking around the room.

"Those who want them do," Harry replied.

"Let's all sit down, then," Andrew suggested. He walked to the couch and sat down.

Bessie joined him, holding her teacup and a plate with a few biscuits on it. After a moment, Doona sat on Andrew's other side. As Bessie settled back in her seat and put her plate down on the small table next to her, the others all found places to sit. Andrew cleared his throat.

"I was telling Bessie, before the rest of you arrived, that Inspector Harrison rang me about an hour ago," he began.

"What time is it in New Zealand?" Doona asked.

Andrew shrugged. "I didn't ask."

"So what's happened?" Harry demanded. "Don't tell me we've solved another case? It felt as if we were still stumbling around in the dark."

"I don't know that we can take credit for this one," Andrew replied. "But there has been a major break in the case, one that we'll be getting at least some credit for, anyway."

"Only some credit?" Ken asked.

Andrew nodded. "After all of our questions about why James had suddenly started speaking to his brother again, Inspector Harrison started keeping a closer eye on James. Yesterday, or maybe it was the day before – the time difference complicates things – he had a constable following James. He told me that he'd done it as much to give the constable a bit of practise as anything else, but when the constable got back to the station, he'd taken a few pictures of James with a woman."

"Amelia?" Doona guessed.

Andrew shook his head. "Janice," he said.

"So they do know one another," John said.

"And the constable was able to get close enough to hear part of their conversation," Andrew continued. "He was unaware of the case, so he didn't understand what they were discussing, but he told Inspector Harrison that James kept telling Janice that she needed to keep her mouth shut and that she must never tell the police who'd told her about the affair."

"That seems a risky conversation to have in a public place," Bessie remarked.

"They met at a restaurant on the outskirts of Auckland," Andrew replied. "The constable was from an Auckland station. James had told Inspector Harrison that he couldn't answer any additional questions for a few days because he needed to travel to Auckland for some meetings. That was when Inspector Harrison assigned someone to follow him."

"And the constable followed him to a meeting with Janice," Bessie said.

"To prove that he was truly going away, James kindly told Inspector Harrison where he would be staying," Andrew told her. "The constable arrived at the hotel just after eight and James walked out of the building twenty minutes later. He met Janice in a coffee shop just a short walk away from the hotel."

"So we now know that James was the one who rang Janice about the affair," Harry said. "It's useful information, but we need a lot more."

"We have some more, anyway," Andrew said. "After Inspector Harrison saw the pictures and heard the constable's report, he flew over to Auckland himself. While he was in the air, he had Janice brought in for questioning."

"I'd have done the same," Harry said.

Andrew nodded. "As soon as Inspector Harrison started to ask her about her morning, she fell apart. She admitted that James was the one who'd rung and told her about the affair. She said she knew it had to be true because James was Larry's brother. She and James had met at a party that Amelia and Larry had given about three months earlier."

"But I thought that James and Larry weren't speaking at that point," Bessie said.

"They weren't. According to Janice, she met James outside on the patio. Amelia had invited him, saying that she hoped he and Larry could make up after their long estrangement. He'd decided to try, but once he'd arrived, he'd hidden himself on the patio, unable to face seeing Larry again."

"And then what happened?" Charles asked.

"According to Janice, she sat and talked to James for an hour, trying to persuade him that he should give Larry another chance. She said she told him all about how she and Amelia were close friends and that Larry was one of the nicest men she knew. Eventually, James decided he couldn't do it and he went home."

"Did she see him or hear from him again after that?" Doona asked.

"She claims that the next time she spoke to him was when he rang to tell her about the affair. She said he started off by reminding her of who he was and then told her that he'd finally overcome his reluctance and contacted Larry. When she said that she was happy for him, he laughed and said that he'd learned a lot about his brother in just a few months and that things were not at all as they appeared."

"Did he tell Janice that Larry was also having an affair, too?" Charles wondered.

THE IRVING FILE

"Apparently not. She told the inspector that James said that he was still thinking through all of the things that he'd learned and that most of them weren't her concern, but that she needed to know one thing. Then he told her about Amelia's affair with Eric. As soon as he'd told her, he made her promise that she'd never tell anyone who'd told her, no matter what happened, ever."

"That covers a lot of ground. If it were me, I'd have worried about that request," Ken said.

"Janice said she was too upset to think straight. She claims she promised him that she'd never tell and then started packing. It wasn't until she learned that Larry was dead that she started to worry about the promise."

"But she still kept it, even knowing that James might have killed Larry," Bessie said.

"Janice claims that she never once considered James a suspect in the case. She told Inspector Harrison that he never would have killed his brother and that she'd kept his secret because James didn't want Amelia to know the truth and be angry with him. For obvious reasons, Janice hasn't spoken to Amelia since the scene at the conference. Inspector Harrison got the impression that she thinks that Amelia and James are together in some way now."

"So James has told her that he's involved with Amelia, and that has kept Janice quiet for all these years," Charles said.

"It certainly seems that way," Andrew replied.

"Now what?" Bessie asked.

"There's a little bit more," Andrew told her. "After he'd spoken to Janice, Inspector Harrison had James brought in for questioning. The inspector started the questioning by asking him how he'd felt when he discovered that Larry was cheating on Amelia. Apparently, James broke down and started shouting about how no one should ever cheat on the most wonderful woman in the world and that once he and Amelia were together, they'd be the happiest couple ever."

"Oh dear," Doona said.

"The inspector stopped the interview when James started ranting about how he'd killed for Amelia and that he'd do it again, if necessary," Andrew added.

"It's all very sad," Bessie said after a long silence.

"It is indeed," Doona agreed.

"And another of our cases gets marked as solved," Harry said. "Even if we didn't exactly solve it."

"We were going in the right direction," Doona argued.

"We were, but I don't know that Janice would ever have admitted to anything under any other circumstances," Andrew said. "Regardless, I'm glad we were able to get justice for Larry."

"The poor man was murdered by his own brother," Hugh said. "Maybe we should have just let Aalish be an only child."

"She is an only child," Doona said.

Hugh flushed. "Until February, anyway."

"My goodness, congratulations!" Bessie exclaimed.

"We aren't really telling anyone yet," Hugh said. "But I kind of just blurted it out."

Everyone offered congratulations, and the party ended on a happy note. Andrew walked Bessie back to her cottage.

"Do you want to get dinner later?" he asked as her door.

"I'd love to get dinner later," she replied. "But first I'm going to open that letter."

Andrew raised an eyebrow.

"I really hope Harlan is exactly who he claims to be, but I'm going to go crazy if I don't know the truth."

"Shall I leave you alone with your results?"

"Oh, no. Please come in and read them with me."

Andrew sat at the kitchen table while Bessie went up and

retrieved the envelope. She sat down across from him and stared at it for a full minute.

"I'm afraid, if he isn't her nephew, that I'm going to feel as if I have to tell Hilary," she said eventually.

"Hilary said she didn't want to know."

"But she ought to know."

"Why?"

Bessie sighed. "You're right, of course. It's her life, and she gets to make her own choices. I'm just sorry that she chose to give me the letter."

Andrew grinned at her. "You don't have to open it."

"Yes, I do."

Bessie tore open the envelope and unfolded the sheet inside. It took her several seconds to decipher the results.

"If I'm right, then Harlan is Hilary's nephew," she said, pushing the sheet towards Andrew.

He read through it and nodded. "The two are definitely related. It sounds as if Cassandra was telling the truth."

Bessie exhaled slowly. "I'm really happy for Hilary."

∽

THREE DAYS LATER, as Bessie was getting ready for a visit to Peel with Helen and Andrew, her telephone rang.

"I told you that Harlan was my nephew," Hilary's voice came down the line.

"Sorry?"

"I told you that Harlan was my nephew. Now you know it's true."

"What makes you think that?"

"There's no way you've gone this long without opening the envelope," Hilary replied with a laugh. "And if you'd opened it and Harlan and I weren't related, you'd have come and told me, even though I told you not to."

"I would have respected your wishes."

"Ah, but that confirms it, anyway."

Bessie laughed. "I'm not sure that anything in that conversation made any sense."

"But Harlan truly is my nephew, isn't he?"

"He is."

"I knew it. I couldn't bring myself to open the envelope, though, so I rather tricked you into doing it. Thank you."

"You're very welcome."

"I won't keep you, but you should know that last night Harlan was surfing the Internet and he found a site all about some sort of experimental treatment for what's wrong with me. We're still looking into it, but if it's half as good as it claims to be, Harlan and I might be flying to America so that I can get treated at a clinic there. Tell your friend that I'm open to offers on the house. I'm hoping for a quick sale so I don't have that to worry about while I'm away."

Bessie put the phone down as Andrew knocked on her door. *I'll have to ring Andy later,* she thought as she pulled on her shoes and headed out with her friends.

THE JORDAN FILE

AN AUNT BESSIE COLD CASE MYSTERY

Release date: June 2, 2023

July brings sunshine and warm weather to the Isle of Man. It also brings Aunt Bessie and her friends another cold case to solve. This time, though, the police may know exactly what happened. It appears that Leo Jordan killed his wife and then himself, but the detective in charge of the case isn't convinced.

While Bessie and the rest of the unit are trying to work out whether the murder/suicide case was actually two murders, Jasper Coventry has problems of his own at the Seaview Hotel.

When one former guest reports having his credit card information stolen while he'd been staying at the Seaview, Jasper is concerned. Days later, the complaints continue to pour in and Jasper is panicking. This sort of thing could seriously damage the luxury hotel's reputation, and he turns to Bessie for help.

Can the cold case unit work out exactly what happened to Leo and Anna Jordan? Can they help Jasper discover which member of his staff has been stealing credit card information from guests? And can Bessie be polite to Dan Ross when it's absolutely necessary?

A SNEAK PEEK AT THE JORDAN FILE

An Aunt Bessie Cold Case Mystery
Release date: June 2, 2023

Please excuse any typos or minor errors. I have not yet completed final edits on this title.

Chapter One

"I can't believe we are actually doing this," Bessie Cubbon said as her friend, Andrew Cheatham, drove them towards Ramsey.

"I'm surprised we've managed to keep the unit quiet for as long as we have," Andrew replied.

"The island does thrive on skeet."

Andrew laughed. "Such a wonderful Manx word."

"It doesn't just mean gossip. It can also mean to have a quick look at something."

"I didn't realise that, but my Manx is seriously limited."

Bessie laughed. "I've taken the introductory Manx class

more times than I want to admit, and my Manx is also seriously limited."

A few minutes later, Andrew drove the car into the Seaview Hotel's large car park. He found a space near the entrance and the pair walked together from the car into the hotel's gorgeous lobby.

"Good afternoon," Sandra Cook said from behind the reception desk. "How are you today?"

"I'll be better after our meeting is over," Bessie said a bit glumly.

Sandra gave her a sympathetic smile. "I was surprised when Mr. Coventry told me who was joining you today."

"Needs must," Andrew told her.

"Mr. Coventry has put you in the penthouse meeting room today," Sandra added. "And he's sent up some extra-nice treats for you as well."

Bessie smiled. "Jasper knows this meeting won't be pleasant."

"I've done everything I could to make it as pleasant as possible," Jasper Coventry said as he walked out of the office behind the reception desk.

He walked around the desk and pulled Bessie into a tight hug. "It isn't too late to sneak out the side door," he whispered in her ear.

Bessie laughed. "It's a tempting thought, but we simply need to get this over with."

Jasper nodded. "In that case, I'll escort you to the penthouse. Your guest has already arrived."

"Of course he has," Bessie muttered as she took the arm that Jasper offered.

"Surely you have better things to do than this," Andrew said to Jasper as they waited for the lift.

"Our summers are very busy, but that doesn't mean that I don't still personally look after my favourite guests," Jasper replied. "What's the point in owning a hotel if you can't take care of your friends?"

"We appreciate everything you do for us," Andrew told him.

"I don't do much, really," Jasper protested.

"You usually spoil us with amazing food for our meetings, even though we're only paying for biscuits and coffee," Andrew countered.

"You're doing very important work, and I feel privileged that you've chosen to have your meetings at the Seaview."

The lift doors opened, and the trio stepped inside the car. As the doors slid shut, Jasper spoke again.

"I'm just sorry that we can't provide rooms for Charles and Harry during the summer months. I hope they are enjoying staying on the beach in Laxey instead."

"They are, very much, actually," Bessie told him. "They both appreciate the extra space that the cottages on the beach provide, but I think they're both looking forward to moving back here in September. I believe they both miss your restaurant and room service."

"And housekeeping," Andrew added. "There's something wonderful about being out all day and coming back to a clean room and a freshly made bed."

Jasper grinned. "We do our best," he said as the lift doors opened again. The threesome walked together to the conference room, where the door was standing open.

"Here we are," Jasper said. "If you need anything, please let me know."

Andrew nodded. "As ever, thank you."

Bessie looked at Andrew and then took a deep breath before she walked into the room. The man sitting at the head of the table looked up from his plate, which was stacked high with cakes and biscuits.

"Ah, I was starting to think no one was actually coming," Dan Ross said with an unpleasant smile.

"We're early," Andrew pointed out as he headed towards the table in the back of the room.

"But I'm a busy man on a deadline," Dan countered. "I have a dozen other places to be, a dozen other stories to write. As the *Isle of Man Times's* only investigative journalist, I'm always in very high demand."

Andrew slowly filled a plate with small cake pieces and biscuits before he replied. "If you need to reschedule our conversation, we can do that," he offered.

Dan shook his head. "I'm just eager to get on with it. I've already written the outline of the article on the cold case unit, but I need a lot more information to finish the piece."

Andrew poured himself a cup of coffee and then walked to the table. Bessie watched, wondering where he'd sit, as he typically sat at the head of the table himself. Andrew didn't hesitate before putting his plate and cup down as far from Dan Ross as he possibly could. Bessie quickly made her own selections from the delicious treats on the table and then put her plate next to Andrew's. She poured herself some tea and then sat down next to him.

"We may as well get started," Dan said. "I know you're a retired Scotland Yard Inspector who has written a number of books about investigative techniques. Why start a cold case unit now?"

Andrew popped a piece of cake into his mouth and chewed it slowly. He washed it down with a sip of coffee before he spoke. "I think it's probably best if we wait to begin until everyone is here," he told Dan.

Dan frowned at his watch and then shrugged. "I hope I don't get called away for anything more important."

I hope he does, Bessie thought. She nibbled on a biscuit as the clock slowly ticked its way to two o'clock.

A SNEAK PEEK AT THE JORDAN FILE

"I thought the meeting was due to start at two," Dan said at one minute past the hour.

Andrew nodded. "I can't imagine what's keeping everyone," he said as he got to his feet. He crossed to the door and pulled it open.

"Ah, there you are," he said to someone just outside of the room.

"We were, um, just chatting," Hugh Watterson said as he walked into the room. Doona Moore and John Rockwell were right behind him. Charles Morris and Harry Blake followed the others. As Andrew shut the door behind them, the new arrivals all gathered around the table at the back of the room.

"I do have other things to do," Dan said loudly as he watched everyone fill plates.

"Don't let us keep you," Doona replied.

Dan flushed. "I was invited to be here today."

"And we're all, um, willing to speak with you," John told him. "Just give us a moment to get some coffee or tea and we'll join you."

Five minutes later, everyone was sitting around the table sipping drinks and eating biscuits and cake. Andrew sighed and then cleared his throat.

"As you all know, I've invited Dan Ross from the *Isle of Man Times* to join us today. He's going to be writing an article for the newspaper about our very unique cold case unit. He'll be including a brief biography of each of the members and a short explanation of the work that we do. We will not be discussing any of the cases we've considered as a unit with him, though."

Dan frowned. "I thought maybe you could tell me about just one, sort of as an example of the kind of work that you do."

Andrew shook his head. "I'm afraid we can't do that. I

will tell you that we consider cases ranging from missing persons to murder and that we've had a much higher success rate than I was expecting us to have when I formed the unit. I'm afraid that's all I'm going to say on the matter."

Dan looked as if he wanted to argue, but after a moment, he simply opened his notebook and made a note. "Okay, where do you want to start?" he asked.

"Introductions?" Andrew suggested.

"Sure," Dan replied. "I already know most of you, but let's pretend I don't."

"I'm Inspector Andrew Cheatham. I'm retired from Scotland Yard. I spent a good deal of my career investigating homicides and other serious crimes. Once I'd retired, I found that I missed the work. A chance conversation with a friend about a cold case got me thinking about starting some sort of cold case unit. This unit is the end result of that random conversation, really. I called in a few favours to get the people that I wanted in the unit, and we've been meeting for several months now."

"And how does the unit work?" Dan asked as Andrew stopped for a sip of his drink.

"We consider a single case each month," Andrew replied. "We start by going through the entire case file from the initial investigation and then work our way through any available updates. Once we've had a chance to consider everything, we send questions to the man or woman who is currently in charge of the investigation. He or she goes back and talks to witnesses again and again, taking new statements and sharing those statements with us."

"And have you managed to solve any cold cases thus far?" Dan asked.

We've solved them all, Bessie thought, shoving a bite of cake into her mouth before she could say anything out loud.

"We've been more successful than I'd expected us to be,"

Andrew told him. "And that's all I'm going to say on the subject."

"My sources suggest that you're being sent cases from all over the world now," Dan said. "My sources told me that lots of people are hoping for your help."

Andrew nodded. "Units like this one are unusual, and there are unsolved cases in every police jurisdiction in the world. There is nothing a police inspector wants more than to solve every case in which he or she is involved, even if that means bringing in outside help."

"But you wouldn't be as in demand if you weren't so successful," Dan suggested.

"When I first set up the unit, I emailed about a half-dozen inspectors I knew from around England," Andrew told him. "Between them, they sent back over a dozen cases that they were interested in having our unit consider. That was before we'd even had our first meeting. Yes, we've had some success, but even if we hadn't solved a single case, we'd still have plenty of cases to consider."

"So why only one a month?" Dan asked.

"Because that's what we can reasonably manage," Andrew told him. "Three of the members of the unit are retired, but all three of us do other consultancy work, too. Two of the members are still working full-time in policing. Another has other business concerns."

"And then there's Bessie," Dan said with a smug smirk.

Bessie flushed. "What does that mean?" she demanded.

"As I understand it, you've never held down a paying job," Dan said. "Surely you have time to look at more than one case a month."

"But we're a unit," Andrew told him. "We work together on each case, one at a time, in a way that's working for us. At the moment, I don't have any plans to change anything."

"How frustrating for the many men and women who need your help," Dan said.

Andrew shrugged. "We do what we can."

Dan nodded. "Right, so you're retired from Scotland Yard, and so are two others in the unit." He looked at Harry. "Harry Blake, I understand you were a homicide inspector, specialising in the most horrific of crimes."

Harry frowned. "That isn't how I would put it," he said stiffly.

"How would you put it, then?" Dan asked.

"I was a homicide inspector, full stop," Harry told him.

"But you did do more than your fair share of investigating the most awful of crimes," Dan said.

"I investigated the cases I was assigned to investigate."

"And now that you've retired, you work with this unit and also as a consultant, working to find serial killers, as I understand it."

"That isn't exactly correct," Harry told him.

"Which part?"

Harry shook his head. "For the purposes of your article on the cold case unit, clarification is unnecessary."

Dan frowned at his notebook. "But I want the article to be as accurate as possible."

"I'm Charles Morris," Charles interrupted. "I'm the other retired inspector in the unit."

Dan stared at Charles for a moment and then looked down at his notebook. "As I understand it, you're an expert at finding missing people," he said eventually. "Is there much demand for that in a cold case unit?"

"We've considered cases that involved missing people," Charles replied.

"And Charles is an expert investigator, no matter what the crime," Andrew added.

Dan made a note. "Were you able to find any of your missing people?" he asked.

"No comment," Andrew said quickly. "I told you we aren't going to discuss the cases we've considered."

"Now that I have the basics, tell me more," Dan said. "I want my readers to get to know you as people. Tell me about your wives, your children, your hobbies, what you like to do with your spare time. Harry, I believe you own a small vineyard in France. Tell me about that."

Harry looked surprised and then slowly shook his head. "No comment," he said tightly.

Bessie exchanged glances with Doona, who looked as surprised as Bessie felt. *How did we not know that Harry owns a vineyard in France?* she wondered. She sat back in her seat, feeling frustrated that, even after several months, she still didn't feel as if she knew Harry or Charles very well.

"Charles, tell me about Mandy," Dan said.

"I don't know what you're talking about," Charles said flatly.

"Of course you do. You must remember Mandy Montgomery. She was your first missing person case, wasn't she? And your first serious girlfriend, as I understand it," Dan said.

"I'll be back when he's gone," Charles said as he got to his feet. He left the room before anyone could reply.

"Wow. I didn't mean to upset him," Dan said, sounding smugly pleased with himself. "Maybe one of you could answer my questions. You all must have heard the story by now."

Bessie frowned. Maybe some of the others had heard the story, but she certainly hadn't.

"I believe you were told that we were going to limit today's interview to brief introductions and a discussion of the cold case unit," Andrew said. "If you can't keep on topic, we can end the interview right now."

"Does that mean you don't want to talk about your wife and children?" Dan asked. "As I understand it, your wife's death wasn't entirely straightforward. I've been told that some of your children still haven't forgiven you for what happened to her."

Andrew opened his mouth to reply and then snapped it shut again. He took a long, deep breath before he spoke again. "As I said, we'll keep the conversation on the cold case unit or end this right now."

Dan shrugged. "Okay, then, what else can you tell me about Charles?"

"I believe he told you everything you need to know," Andrew countered. "You need to meet everyone else in the unit."

Dan laughed. "Oh, but I know everyone else. Police Inspector John Rockwell, who runs the police station in Laxey. His wife died under mysterious circumstances, too, but I don't suppose anyone wants to talk about that, either."

John gave Dan a cool smile. "Sue and I were divorced, and she was married to another man when she passed away while on her honeymoon. If you have questions about what happened to her, you should talk to her second husband."

Dan nodded. "I'd love to talk to him. I've left dozens of messages for him at every number I have for him, but he never rings me back."

"He's a busy man," John said flatly.

"As I understand it, he's actually doing some good work in Africa," Dan said. "Even if he is mostly hiding there so that he doesn't have to answer any questions about what happened to Sue."

John shrugged. "He's been interviewed by the local police."

A SNEAK PEEK AT THE JORDAN FILE

"And you've been left to raise two teenagers on your own," Dan said. "How is that going?"

"I love my children and I'm very proud of them. They've had a lot to deal with over the past few years and they're both doing great, regardless," John said.

"It must help that you have a new woman in your life, too," Dan said. "Although I'm not clear on exactly when you and Doona became involved. Someone told me that you were already sleeping together before your divorce."

Doona inhaled sharply. "Your someone gave you the wrong information," she said angrily. "Not that it's any of your business."

John put a hand on her arm. "I believe we're meant to be talking about the cold case unit," he said.

Andrew nodded. "And if you ask more inappropriate questions, this conversation is over," he warned Dan.

Dan grinned at him and made a note. "Okay, so John Rockwell is currently with the local island police. So is Hugh Watterson." He nodded at Hugh. "How does a lowly constable end up on a cold case unit with four inspectors?"

"Hugh is an excellent investigator who is working hard to advance his career," Andrew replied. "He also works well with the other members of the unit, and I was delighted to be able to include him when I was putting the unit together."

"You're in school, aren't you?" Dan asked Hugh. "I'm surprised you have time to study, with a wife and a baby at home. Between work, school, and this unit, you must never see baby Alice."

"Her name is Aalish, and I spend as much time with her as I possibly can," Hugh told him. "And none of that is relevant to today's conversation."

"Of course, I'm not certain how Doona can run a UK holiday park from the island, either," Dan said. "What a wonderful inheritance, though. Such a shame your husband had to die so tragically in order for you to become a millionaire."

Bessie was surprised when Doona chuckled.

"I'm beyond caring what you think of me, Dan," she said.

"Does it worry you that John Rockwell only started chasing after you once you became rich?" Dan asked.

Doona and John exchanged glances and then they both burst out laughing.

"Not at all," Doona said eventually. "But you're wandering off topic again."

Dan looked down at his notebook. "That just leaves Bessie, of course. Elizabeth Cubbon, known as Aunt Bessie to nearly everyone. Age unknown, or rather, unacknowledged, although my sources suggest that she's well past eighty. Bessie is another one who inherited a fortune, decades ago now. She used the money to buy herself a cottage on Laxey Beach and she's been living there ever since. What must it be like to inherit so much money that you never have to work a day in your life? I'd love to find out."

"You've already worked for a great many years," Bessie pointed out.

Dan frowned. "You know what I mean."

"Again, you're quite far away from what we're meant to be discussing," Andrew said. "If you don't have any more questions about the cold case unit, we can wrap this up."

"How do you choose which cases you consider?" Dan asked.

"I get emails every day from people who want us to consider cases. I read brief summaries of every case that is suggested, and then I request more information on the ones that interest me. I try to focus on cases where I feel things were missed, but, at the end of the day, it often just comes down to random choice," Andrew explained.

Dan looked up from his notebook. "You make all of the selections?"

"I have so far. That may change in the future," Andrew told him.

"Tell me something about the case you're going to be considering this month," Dan suggested.

Andrew shook his head. "I'm afraid I can't do that."

As Dan opened his mouth to reply, loud music began to play somewhere. Dan frowned and pulled out his mobile. He glanced at it and then sighed. "I need to answer this," he said as he got to his feet and headed for the door. He started talking immediately.

"What?" He sighed.

"Right now?" Dan made a face. "Surely someone else…"

"I'll be there in ten minutes," he said after a brief pause.

"I have to go," Dan said as he turned around before he reached the door. He dropped his mobile back into his pocket and then walked back to pick up his notebook and pen. "Thank you for your time thus far. When can we continue?"

"I think you have everything you need for your article," Andrew replied. "If you have any additional questions, why don't you just ring me?"

Dan clearly wanted to argue, but his mobile began to ring again before he could speak. Frowning, he pulled out the device and headed for the door.

"I'll ring you," he shouted over his shoulder as he left the room, his mobile to his ear.

ALSO BY DIANA XARISSA

The Isle of Man Cozy Mysteries

Aunt Bessie Assumes
Aunt Bessie Believes
Aunt Bessie Considers
Aunt Bessie Decides
Aunt Bessie Enjoys
Aunt Bessie Finds
Aunt Bessie Goes
Aunt Bessie's Holiday
Aunt Bessie Invites
Aunt Bessie Joins
Aunt Bessie Knows
Aunt Bessie Likes
Aunt Bessie Meets
Aunt Bessie Needs
Aunt Bessie Observes
Aunt Bessie Provides
Aunt Bessie Questions
Aunt Bessie Remembers
Aunt Bessie Solves
Aunt Bessie Tries
Aunt Bessie Understands
Aunt Bessie Volunteers
Aunt Bessie Wonders

Aunt Bessie's X-Ray
Aunt Bessie Yearns
Aunt Bessie Zeroes In

The Aunt Bessie Cold Case Mysteries

The Adams File
The Bernhard File
The Carter File
The Durand File
The Evans File
The Flowers File
The Goodman File
The Howard File
The Irving File
The Jordan File

The Markham Sisters Cozy Mystery Novellas

The Appleton Case
The Bennett Case
The Chalmers Case
The Donaldson Case
The Ellsworth Case
The Fenton Case
The Green Case
The Hampton Case
The Irwin Case
The Jackson Case
The Kingston Case

The Lawley Case
The Moody Case
The Norman Case
The Osborne Case
The Patrone Case
The Quinton Case
The Rhodes Case
The Somerset Case
The Tanner Case
The Underwood Case
The Vernon Case
The Walters Case
The Xanders Case
The Young Case
The Zachery Case

The Janet Markham Bennett Cozy Thrillers

The Armstrong Assignment
The Blake Assignment
The Carlson Assignment
The Doyle Assignment
The Everest Assignment
The Farnsley Assignment
The George Assignment
The Hamilton Assignment
The Ingram Assignment

The Isle of Man Ghostly Cozy Mysteries

Arrivals and Arrests
Boats and Bad Guys
Cars and Cold Cases
Dogs and Danger
Encounters and Enemies
Friends and Frauds
Guests and Guilt
Hop-tu-Naa and Homicide
Invitations and Investigations
Joy and Jealousy
Kittens and Killers
Letters and Lawsuits
Marsupials and Murder
Neighbors and Nightmares
Orchestras and Obsessions
Proposals and Poison
Questions and Quarrels
Roses and Revenge
Secrets and Suspects
Theaters and Threats
Umbrellas and Undertakers
Visitors and Victims
Weddings and Witnesses
Xylophones and X-Rays
Yachts and Yelps

The Sunset Lodge Mysteries

The Body in the Annex

The Body in the Boathouse
The Body in the Cottage

The Lady Elizabeth Cozies in Space

Alibis in Alpha Sector
Bodies in Beta Sector
Corpses in Chaos Sector

The Midlife Crisis Mysteries

Anxious in Nevada
Bewildered in Florida

The Isle of Man Romances

Island Escape
Island Inheritance
Island Heritage
Island Christmas

The Later in Life Love Stories

Second Chances
Second Act
Second Thoughts
Second Degree
Second Best
Second Nature
Second Place

BOOKPLATES ARE NOW AVAILABLE

Would you like a signed bookplate for this book?

I now have bookplates (stickers) that I can personalize, sign, and send to you. It's the next best thing to getting a signed copy!

Send an email to diana@dianaxarissa.com with your mailing address (I promise not to use it for anything else, ever) and how you'd like your bookplate personalized and I'll sign one and send it to you.

There is no charge for a bookplate, but there is a limit of one per person.

ABOUT THE AUTHOR

Diana has been self-publishing since 2013, and she feels surprised and delighted to have found readers who enjoy the stories and characters that she imagines. Always an avid reader, she still loves nothing more than getting lost in fictional worlds, her own or others!

After being raised in Erie, Pennsylvania, and studying history at Allegheny College in Meadville, Pennsylvania, Diana pursued a career in college administration. She was living and working in Washington, DC, when she met her future husband, an Englishman who was visiting the city.

Following her marriage, Diana moved to Derbyshire. A short while later, she and her husband relocated to the Isle of Man. After ten years on the island, during which Diana earned a Master's degree in the island's history, they made the decision to relocate again, this time to the US.

Now living near Buffalo, New York, Diana and her husband live with their daughter, a student at the University at Buffalo. Their son is now living and working just outside of Boston, Massachusetts, giving Diana an excuse to travel now and again.

Diana also writes mystery/thrillers set in the not-too-distant future as Diana X. Dunn and Young Adult fiction as D.X. Dunn.

She is always happy to hear from readers. You can write to her at:

Diana Xarissa Dunn
PO Box 72
Clarence, NY 14031.

Find Diana at: DianaXarissa.com
E-mail: Diana@dianaxarissa.com

Made in the USA
Columbia, SC
18 May 2024